What Readers Are Saying About
SPEAK TENDERLY TO HER

"Ruth Griffin has beautifully rewritten and modernized the biblical story of Hosea and Gomer. Life is full of heartache and bad choices. But love and forgiveness can heal all."

"Speak Tenderly To Her speaks to the heart in an unforgettable way. It's a love story worth telling!"

"Nicely written love story. It makes you think about your own relationship, and how easy it is to focus on what's wrong rather than what is right."

"An awesome read!"

Other Books By The Author

After The Call

Stay With Me

Stepmother's Anonymous

The Book of Joy

Ruth E. Griffin

SPEAK Tenderly TO HER

Studio Griffin
A Publishing Company
www.studiogriffin.net

For information, contact:
Studio Griffin
A Publishing Company
studiogriffin@outlook.com
www.studiogriffin.net

Cover Design by Ruth E. Griffin
Image by © Lightfield Studios / Adobe

First Edition

ISBN-13: 978-0-578-52179-4

3 4 5 6 7 8 9 10

SPEAK Tenderly TO HER

For my family

"To forgive is the highest,
most beautiful form of love."
Robert Muller

One

"**S**HE SAID 'THANK YOU'," Janice stated as she approached Dr. Tory Jamison. She was usually stoic in her duties at the pediatric clinic. Not today though—today her eyes were glistening with unshed tears.

"Who did?" he asked.

"Hannah," the nurse replied, referring to the rambunctious toddler who spent as much time at the clinic as the doctors and nurses who treated her.

"So... what?" he said.

"She thanked me for giving her a shot," the nurse exclaimed. "What child does that? She makes me want to cry for hurting her."

"You're getting soft in your old age," he ribbed as she handed him Hannah's chart. The little girl was his final patient of the day, and then he was gone. He had a date to get ready for—a date with the *beautiful* Officer Rebecca Garner, with long, blonde hair and baby-blue eyes. She was taller than his five-foot-ten frame, but this didn't bother him at all. She was perfect, and he was looking forward to spending time with her.

Tory walked over to the Hannah's room, knocked, and then entered. Her mother,

Ashley, a young woman in her mid-twenties, was struggling to keep the girl on the examination table and quickly losing the battle. Hannah twisted her body to the side and slid between her mother and the table, landing with an abrupt thud on the hard floor. She swiftly crawled out of her mother's grasp, not realizing Tory was in her path.

"And where are you going?" he asked, dropping the chart on the table and picking her up. She fought his hold on her until she realized who it was, then she squealed and reached into his breast pocket. She dug in deep but came up empty. She frowned, confused—this was where he usually kept the lollipops he offered to his patients at the end of their visit. Instead Tory pulled one out of his pants pocket and held it up.

"Is this what you're looking for?"

She squealed again and grabbed the treat, wasting no time in pulling off the wrapper. Tory set her down with a smile. He viewed at all his patients as *his* kids, but of them, Hannah was his favorite. Ashley brought her in almost a year earlier for a skin infection that wouldn't go away. He diagnosed her with eczema and began treatment to get the illness under control. Some days were better than others, but for the most part she learned to live with the constant itching and irritation.

What impressed Tory the most about Hannah was her spirit; she was a fighter and didn't let anything stop her. Unfortunately, this often resulted in unplanned trips to the emergency room.

Tory turned to her mother and handed her a prescription.

"Let's see how she does with this cream. Call me if you don't see a change."

Ashley offered him a weary smile and said, "Thank you, Dr. Jamison."

He smiled warmly and exited the room.

TORY WHISTLED as he weaved through traffic on his bicycle. He owned a car, but because he lived only a few miles from the clinic, he chose to ride his bike. If he was feeling really ambitious, he could walk to work, but as it was, he was grateful he didn't have to sit in traffic.

He thought about Rebecca. He was on-call at the hospital the night they met. One of his patients had to be transported to the hospital via ambulance and she had accompanied them. He took note of her as she came in with the family, but it was only when the emergency was over, when Rebecca inquired about the patient, that he fully appreciated her features: her beautiful face, hour-glass figure, and a smile that seemed to brighten up whatever room she was in. She could have easily been a swimsuit model, which was reason enough to hesitate when it came to asking her out, but eventually Tory did and now they were going to go on their first date.

Tory turned into his street, still whistling. *You are such a dork,* he thought to himself, as he arrived at the apartment complex. He had lived there for the past ten years and though he thought to move several times, he never did. His apartment was big enough for him; he didn't need any more space and it was a plus he didn't have to worry about yard work. Perhaps one day he'd have a reason to move, but until then he was content right where he was.

Tory was getting his mail out of the central mailboxes when he saw *her* sitting on the bench outside his apartment.

Isobel.

He stopped walking, stopped thinking and for a minute, he even stopped breathing. Only his heart continued to beat, hard, as Isobel raised her head and met his gaze. Her light brown eyes seemed to soak in the light around them and shine as the sun itself. Her dark brown hair was short the last time he saw her, but it had grown out, covering her shoulders and falling softly to her back. She had always been petite, but she had gained weight, giving her a full look that enhanced her figure to radiate sensuality.

Oh, what the hell am I thinking? he thought, giving himself a mental kick. She left him, and here he was thinking how good she looked?

"Tory!"

He broke eye contact with Isobel and turned to the older gentleman approaching him. It was Pastor Martin, his minister, a stocky, solid fellow who spent the first half of his life in the Navy. While traces of his former life slipped into his conversation every once in a while, there was no doubt whom he served now, which worried Tory.

"What's going on?" he asked, bypassing a greeting. Given the fact that Isobel was sitting at his front door after leaving four years earlier, Tory didn't want to waste time patty-caking around the issue.

"Well how's that for a how-do-you-do?" the older man said, placing a hand on Tory's shoulder. "But I appreciate your candor, so I won't beat around the bush. Isobel came to me earlier today needing help. She's been through a lot and just needs a place to stay. We've got her on a waiting list at the mission, but nothing is available now. I'm asking you to take her in, just for a couple of weeks, until a bed opens up."

Tory had been listened as the man spoke but wasn't sure he heard him right.

"You want me to take her in?"

"Yes."

Pastor Martin didn't flinch, neither did he apologize.

Tory shook his head.

"You've got some balls asking me to do that." He should have been more respectful towards the man but considering the hell he had gone through with Isobel, he didn't feel too reverential at the moment.

"So, I've been told," Pastor Martin said, a hint of humor in his voice.

The minister's calm, almost indifferent attitude irritated him.

"I can't believe you, of all people, would ask that of me," Tory said, raising his voice. He didn't care if Isobel heard—in fact, he hoped she did. She didn't deserve his help, and by the look on her face it seemed she knew it too. He noted her body language, her shame-filled disposition, and knew she was close to tears. *Good*, he thought. "You know what she did," he added.

"Yes. She left. You're right. But she's changed. She's not the woman she used to be and given the fact that she is a child of God, like you are, we can't turn our backs on her."

Tory wasn't moved by the minister's induction of God into the conversation. Obviously, the man wished to guilt him into letting her stay, but that wasn't going to happen.

"I can. Find someone else."

Tory started around the pastor, but the older man wouldn't give up. He took hold of Tory's elbow with enough force to stop him. Tory set the kickstand on the bike and turned back to his pastor.

"I said, find someone else," he said with more conviction. "I'm not doing this for her."

"Someone like who, Tory?"

"I don't know, and to be honest, I don't care. She's been gone four years. Ask her. I'm sure there were other men. Maybe one of them will help," he returned with all the anger and resentment that had accumulated in the past few years.

Pastor Martin was unfazed by the remark. He turned his back to Isobel and said, his voice considerably lower, "I know she hurt you when she left..."

Tory opened his mouth to correct him, to tell him that he was over her and didn't want anything to do with the situation, but Pastor Martin held his hand up.

"I'm not excusing what she did. You're a good man, Tory, and these past four years have not been easy. I understand that. But I am coming to you as a man who is responsible for others. I'm not asking you to do this for her, but for me. I'm asking you to help me by helping her. You work at the clinic. You see people every day who are often one day, one paycheck, one wrong decision away from poverty. I see families who are living on the streets, living in their cars, that I have to turn away because I have no room, or I lack the resources. It breaks my heart to do so and if I have a chance to help someone, then I will find a way to do it. Please."

The man wasn't wrong. The clinic, which was located on the hospital campus, provided medical services to low- and no-income patients and families. Including Hannah. Her mom was a single mother who worked overnights to make ends meet, and because that wasn't enough, she had to rely on public assistance to pay for the ever-increasing medical visits that resulted from Hannah's condition and her unstoppable zeal for life. Knowing their situation, Tory determined long ago he would bend over backwards to make sure Ashley and Hannah stayed off the streets. What Pastor Martin was asking of him was no different.

But it was Isobel he was asking for.

You can't turn your back on her..., came the voice in the back of his mind.

She was the one who turned her back on me, he argued back.

Look at her; she's scared. You have to let her stay...

Tory gazed back at Isobel. Her head was hanging low. Her cheeks were flushed, and it was apparent that she was embarrassed. Isobel was finally reaping what she had sowed.

But no one, not even her, deserved to live on the streets.

Dammit, he thought and sighed with disgust. As much as he wanted to walk away, he couldn't just leave her sitting there on the bench.

He shook his head and turned back to Pastor Martin.

"Fine," he muttered.

The older man smiled and clasped his hand on Tory's shoulder. His grip was tight, reminding Tory of the years he spent in the military; even after retiring, the man was still a formidable force. There was no way Tory could have said 'no' to him.

Pastor Martin walked by him to talk to Isobel, who rose as he approached. Tory watched her, unsure of what he was feeling.

Anger? Definitely. Compassion? Hardly. Fear... Fear? Of what? Isobel leaving again? No, on the contrary, he thanked God this would only be for two weeks.

Tory turned back to his bike. He kicked the stand up and walked it to the front door. Pastor Martin picked up Isobel's bag and placed his arm around her shoulders, almost nudging her forward. Tory unlocked the front door and carried his bike over the threshold into the foyer where he parked it. He walked into the small kitchen, dropped his bag on the counter, and turned around to face them.

Isobel quietly took a few steps into the kitchen with Pastor Martin behind her. He walked past her and offered Tory his hand.

"Thank you, Tory," he said sincerely.

"Two weeks, right?" Tory asked as he took the man's hand.

"That's all. I'll call you and keep you updated," he returned.

Tory acknowledged him and escorted him to the door. Pastor Martin thanked him again and left.

Only when he latched the door did the reality of the situation set it. He was alone with Isobel. For two weeks. Tory took a deep breath and turned around.

Isobel remained where she stopped in the kitchen, her gaze set on the floor. She seemed humbler, quieter, and dejected—hardly the woman he once knew. She had changed for sure.

Tory cleared his throat.

"You know where everything is," he muttered, and started around Isobel. She backed up as he came close to her, like she was afraid of him. He rolled his eyes and brushed past her quickly.

Tory was halfway to his bedroom when he heard her call his name. He stopped walking but didn't turn around.

"I'm...sorry," she said softly. "I didn't want to come here...I mean, after everything that happened...I'm sorry."

Tory shook his head and continued walking. He slammed the door to his room and leaned back against the wall, inhaling deeply. This was a bad idea, a very bad idea. If he had to be around her for two weeks while she dredged up the past, he was going to lose his mind. He would just have to stay gone, starting with tonight.

Without another thought, Tory grabbed a fresh change of clothes and went back out into the hallway to the bathroom. Tory quickly showered up, dressed, grabbed his keys and wallet, and left. He didn't see Isobel, so he assumed she had already made herself at home in the spare bedroom. Hopefully she'd stay there.

He drove around for a while before settling on a pub downtown that he frequented when he was out with friends. Tonight though, it was just him and he was glad—he didn't want to justify his decision to anyone.

Two

A S SOON AS TORY SHUT THE door to the bathroom, Isobel picked up her bag and walked back to the spare bedroom. She looked around the space that would be hers for the next two weeks and sighed. It looked more like a storage closet than a bedroom. There was a vacuum in the corner, a saw on the desk and beside it, two trash cans filled with wrapping paper. Boxes were piled up everywhere, filled with old medical books, household items, towels, paints, brushes and dishes. There was even a box of her stuff, items she left behind.

Isobel placed her bag on the floor and moved over to the bed where her box was. It was mostly clothes, but she recalled them rather fondly: the little black dress she was wearing the night she met Tory; the turtleneck that was too big but she kept because he bought it for her; the t-shirts from vacation spots they never went to. There were also books, pictures, and a couple of stuffed animals, among other things. This was what her life amounted to, and it all fit in this box.

How strange it felt to be home again.

But this wasn't her home anymore. She— a vagabond who was about eight, maybe ten weeks pregnant—was just passing through. She was still shocked by the news and could only imagine how Tory would have reacted had he known. She didn't tell Pastor Martin about it and she was glad. She didn't know he would go to Tory. As her former minister, she had gone to him for help and nothing more.

"So, are you back for good? Or just traveling through?" he had asked her.

Isobel took a deep breath.

"To be honest, I don't know. I got into…a situation… and I don't have anywhere else to turn. I just need a place to stay for a few weeks, just 'til I can get something together. I could work, I could clean, I'll do whatever it takes, and I thought you could help me—"

"Whoa, Isobel," Pastor Martin said. "Slow down."

Isobel swallowed the lump in her throat and looked down to her hands. She had been wringing them as she spoke and didn't realize it until she saw how red they were. Why was this so hard? This was her pastor He understood. He had always encouraged her, even when she didn't accept his advice. So why couldn't she do this now without getting so nervous?

Because she was admitting guilt. She was telling him how wrong she was and how right he'd been. She had failed, and this was just confirmation.

"Are you okay? You look healthy, but is everything okay?"

She heard the concern in his voice and fought the urge to cry. She nodded.

"Good, good. I'm so glad to see you. I've worried for you all these years and prayed you were alright. This wasn't the way I hoped you'd return, but the important thing is that you're back."

They continued talking about the ministries available at the church. She had never volunteered, but she was aware of what they did to help others, to help those in her same position. As she listened, she found herself distracted, thinking about Tory. *It's only natural,* she thought to herself. This had been their church when she was still there. Not that they attended often, they were busy; he began working at the ER and spending a lot of time at the hospital, while she justified her reasons for wanting to leave.

"Isobel."

She looked up at the sound of her name.

"You look like you're a million miles away," he said.

"I was just...," she began. Should she ask? Why not? What was one more question? She looked back down to her hands, which were wringing again on their own. She stopped and lay them out on her knees. "I was just wondering," she started again, enunciating each word, "how Tory is doing."

Did Tory move? Did he become bitter? Stop going to church? Change from the sweet, caring man he used to be, or worse than all that, did he find someone else?

When Pastor Martin didn't immediately respond, she looked up. He was smiling.

"He's been good. Busy, like always," he said. "The last few years haven't been easy, but he's managed. He works at the hospital clinic now. In pediatrics."

She nodded and turned back to her hands. Tory had always been good with kids; they had even talked about becoming parents. Or rather, he had talked, and she had balked. At least part of his dream was at last realized.

Isobel didn't say anything else as tears fell steadily down her face. She didn't mean to cry—she just did.

Pastor Martin spoke softly.

"Isobel, we all make mistakes. We all have regrets. We need to recognize them for what they are and move forward. Put the past behind you. Your childhood. Your marriage. Your divorce. All you can do now is move forward."

It wasn't an important detail, but Isobel still corrected him.

"We're still married," she said between sniffles. She ran her hand over her face to wipe the tears. She was a grown woman for God's sake, she should be able to control her emotions.

"What do you mean?"

Isobel looked up at him.

"About what?

He grabbed some tissues from his desk and handed them to her.

"What you said; you're still married?"

She nodded, wiping her eyes.

"I didn't bother with a divorce because I just wanted to leave," she explained, refolding her tissues, "but Tory didn't pursue it either."

Pastor Martin raised an eyebrow and looked at her thoughtfully.

"Is that so?"

She nodded, not knowing what else to say. Her tears ceased and she watched him, unsure of what to make of his reaction. There was a twinkle in his eye and his mind seemed to be racing.

After a moment, he sat back and cleared his throat.

"Well, like I was saying, we've extended our homeless ministry in the time you were gone but unfortunately there are a lot of people, a lot of women with children who are in situations like yours. We do have a food pantry and job training programs, but shelter-wise, the best I can do now is to put you on a waiting list until a bed opens up."

Isobel sank into her chair. What was she going to do now?

"However, I think we can find you a place to stay for a couple of weeks until something opens up."

She gazed into his eyes, hopeful.

"Where?"

SETTING THE box aside, Isobel sat down on the bed. Even though she vehemently argued against it, Pastor Martin insisted on talking to Tory about letting her stay with him. He still cared for her, he argued. He was a good man who would not let someone sleep on the streets, he said. He volunteered all the time and would most certainly help.

Yet she heard Tory. He said no, and not just once. He didn't want her there. It wasn't until Pastor Martin shamed him into changing his mind that he agreed.

Isobel looked around the room. What was she thinking? She had no business being here and if Tory knew she was pregnant, he would put her out in a heartbeat. She deserved that and much more, but she had no other options.

A few of nights of sleeping on the streets had cured her of her pride and if it meant she had to justly endure Tory's bitterness and anger, then she would, if only for the sake of her child.

Her mind inadvertently went back to Tory. She had been anxious all the way to the apartment, to the place that used to be her home. Pastor Martin was rambling on about something, but she didn't hear a word of it. How would she feel when she saw Tory? Would she cry? Would she beg his forgiveness? Or would she simply throw up? Thankfully she hadn't experienced any morning sickness, but the way her stomach was feeling then, she knew she wouldn't be able to keep anything down.

When he finally came home, when she finally saw him walking up to his apartment, her stomach fluttered, but not because she was sick. No, something curious happened; her heart ached the same way it used to when they were newlyweds. Her skin flushed at the sight of his green eyes and she couldn't help but stare at his fit body. He needed a haircut badly, his shaggy, dark hair falling over his forehead, but he was still so handsome. She wanted to run her hands through his hair and kiss his soft lips.

Tory no longer belonged to her though and she was not the person she used to be. Life had been a hard teacher, leaving her a quiet, scared, and humbled version of the person she once was. She was also heavier now, and not just because she was pregnant; she had gained thirty-five pounds and it all settled on her hips and her thighs. Her hair was longer and unmanageable. Her face was freckled and lacked the luster it once held. Whatever Tory ever saw in her was gone, and she hated who she had become.

The slam of the front door brought her back to her reality.

Tory had left.

Part of her was upset that he felt the need to avoid her, but the rest of her was relieved. She didn't want to be reminded of her guilt and instead focused on the present. She knew she had to clean up the room and make it livable, but first, she needed to get something to eat. She hadn't eaten anything since that morning, and she was feeling queasy.

Isobel made her way to the kitchen and opened the fridge, only to find it lacking sustenance. There were a couple of beers, some milk, half a loaf of bread, leftover takeout burger and exactly three lemons. The cabinets weren't much better; they were filled with corn flakes, coffee, sugar, syrup and a couple boxes of rice mixes. It was a pitiful sight, but it was more than what she had. She grabbed what was left of the burger and the milk and sat down at the counter to eat. Hopefully Tory wouldn't miss it.

She glanced around the apartment as she chewed on the cold meat. It wasn't as cluttered as her bedroom, but it wasn't exactly neat either. She guessed he only came home to sleep, and if that was indeed the case, then she probably wouldn't be seeing much of him in the next two weeks.

Her stomach now full, Isobel disposed of the container and noted how messy the kitchen was: dirty dishes in the sink, cold coffee in the pot, crumbs all over the place. She didn't remember Tory being this messy, but then that was four years ago. People change in a lot less time, she reminded herself.

Without thinking twice, she filled the sink with hot, soapy water, and started to scrub the dishes. When she finished cleaning, she dried her hands and went to find some clean sheets for her bed. The linen closet beside the restroom was empty, but she smiled, knowing just where to look. Tory had a habit of starting laundry but not finishing it. He would often leave his damp clothes in the washer for days before remembering they were in there, only to have to wash them again. On the occasion that he did actually remember to dry the clothes and get them out of the dryer, he had the tendency to leave the laundry basket in the closet, or the hallway, without putting anything away. It was annoying when they were married, but it seemed endearing now.

Isobel's countenance dropped; it was only endearing because it was familiar, not because there was anything left between them.

She checked the dryer and sure enough, the bed sheets were in there. The fresh laundered smell was gone, but they were clean. She picked a couple for her bed, folded the rest, and put them where they belonged. The least she could do to show her gratitude was clean up. She wasn't sure he would appreciate it, but she would do it anyway.

Isobel spent the next hour moving boxes, fixing her bed, and wondering if Tory would eventually come home—not that she cared, she just didn't want him to feel put out. Tired, she finally curled up on her bed and fell asleep.

Several hours later she awoke to a loud noise. She was startled for a moment, disoriented even, forgetting where she was. But soon it all came back, and she realized it was Tory making the ruckus. She couldn't see much, it was still dark outside, but she knew it was late; she also knew that based on the way Tory was stumbling about, he was drunk.

Isobel remained still on the bed, her eyes fixed on the door. She had left it cracked before going to sleep and watched as Tory went into his bedroom. She couldn't remember a time she had seen him drink so much. Tory was always even-tempered, balanced, and sober. But again, that was four years ago.

Rolling over to face the wall, she didn't want to think about what she had done to him. She needed some sleep and then when she got up in the morning, she was going to do whatever necessary to put the past behind her. She didn't know what that would entail, but she would figure it out.

Try as she could though, Isobel couldn't go back to sleep. She tossed and turned for several hours before abandoning the hope of rest to get up and shower. She grabbed one of the towels in her room, her hygiene kit, and made her way to the bathroom, tiptoeing so as not to wake Tory.

Isobel didn't plan to linger in the shower, but when the hot water hit her, it felt so comforting. She relaxed as the streams massaged her back and gave her a sense of renewal. She could start this day, having washed everything else off.

She was drying herself off when the door suddenly opened. It was Tory. Startled, she screamed and frantically reached for her towel as he apologized and shut the door. Isobel's heart continued to race even after she wrapped the towel tightly around her. She wasn't prudish, nor was she shy, and she wasn't showing enough for him to figure out she was pregnant; she just didn't want him to see the bruises on her legs and on her back.

Three

TORY'S HEAD POUNDED AS HE dragged himself out of bed. He wanted to bury himself in his blankets and not get up until the churning in his stomach subsided, but his bladder was calling—no, it was yelling—for attention. If he didn't do something about it, he was going to be swimming in his sheets. He stumbled through his doorway, into the hall, and to the bathroom. It seemed strange that the light should be shining from beneath the door, or that the exhaust fan should be on, but he didn't make much of it until he opened the door.

The first thing to assault his senses was the light—it was much too bright for this hour. The second thing was the scream. Alarmed, he looked up to see Isobel standing there, naked, trying to cover herself with her towel.

Isobel? This was a dream, right? She was gone, but here she was, back in his apartment, in his bathroom, stark naked.

No, it wasn't a dream. It was real—she was back, and he had walked in on her.

Tory forgot about his bladder, muttered an apology, and shut the door. He leaned back against the wall and took a deep breath, remembering now the events of the previous evening…how Isobel had returned…how she was staying with him for two weeks…how she had a beautiful body…

He had always found her attractive, but now she was voluptuous and enticing; there was just something about her that begged for him to touch her.

But there were bruises on her back and her legs. Seeing this was enough to remind him, among other things, that whatever her situation was, he didn't want to know. He only wanted to make it through these two weeks and forget her.

Isobel opened the door after a few minutes and slunk back to her room without looking at him. Tory was instantly annoyed. They had been married long enough that she needn't act so prim around him. Was she too good for him now?

After emptying his bladder, Tory went back to bed. He didn't sleep very long though; years of getting up early had robbed him of his ability to sleep in. He decided to get up and found Isobel in the kitchen—his clean kitchen—making toast. She offered him a cup of coffee, black, just like he drank it, and apologized. "It's all I could find."

Tory didn't respond, neither did he look at her. He grabbed the mug and walked back to his room. It was Sunday, his day off and he didn't want to spend it with her. He knew he should have been getting ready to go to church, but after spending the night drinking, it was the last place he wanted to be.

He took a sip of the hot drink and instantly felt better. His head still hurt, but not as bad as it did earlier. After another sip, Tory set the mug on the bedside table and lay back down on the bed, throwing the pillow over his head.

His mobile phone rang, the tone loud and grating. He fumbled around on the nightstand to find it and silence it. It wasn't on the table though. The phone rang again. He lifted his head and looked around. The phone was nowhere. It rang again from his back pocket. He groaned and pulled it out.

"Yeah," he muttered, dropping back on the bed. He pulled the pillow over his face, hoping to God this wasn't an emergency. He was in no shape to function on a basic human level, let alone go to the hospital.

"You know, I've experienced lots of things in my life, but never being stood up."

Rebecca!

Tory sat up quickly, a sharp pain stabbing him in the temple. He cradled his head with his free hand and leaned forward.

"God, Rebecca," he muttered, his voice hoarse. "I am so sorry."

"I hope so. Do you know what it's like waiting on someone who's not coming?" she asked; and though her words were meant as a reprimand, he could hear the humor in them. Tory smiled appreciatively; even without knowing what happened, she seemed understanding.

"Listen, I can't apologize enough. I was looking forward to seeing you, I swear, but something came up at the last minute. I...well, it was...it was an emergency. Family." Tory stumbled through his apology, not really wanting to explain about Isobel. Fortunately, Rebecca didn't press the issue.

"Is everything okay now?"

He paused. He wouldn't call it okay, but again, he didn't want to explain.

"Yeah, we're cool now," he muttered.

"Good. So, when are you going to make it up to me?"

Tory could hear her smile as she spoke.

"Are you off today?" he asked. "Maybe we could go out this afternoon."

"What'd did you have in mind?"

Tory thought for a moment. Eating, if he could stomach something. Movies, maybe. What else was there? And why did thinking make his brain hurt so much?

"Lady's choice, since I stood you up," he finally said.

Rebecca laughed.

"What a cop-out!" she said, reading his thoughts.

"Oh, you hurt me," Tory groaned, "I was thinking of you and your feelings and that's what I get?"

"Don't even try that," she said, unconvinced. "But because I like you, I will let it slide this time. Besides, I know a cool place. I'll pick you up around four, okay?"

Perfect. He could sleep the rest of his hangover off.

"Yes, ma'am," he told her and hung up. He buried himself back under his pillow, blocking out the daylight and thought about Rebecca as he drifted off back to sleep.

When Tory woke up, his head wasn't pounding as much. He took some pain medicine and found he could function again. Back to the kitchen to get more coffee, Tory might have forgotten again that he had a houseguest, except for the sudden cleanliness of the place. He should have been grateful, but it only annoyed him. What was she trying to say? That he was a slob and she couldn't stay there without cleaning up after him? He didn't ask her to. She needed to stay out of his life and focus on hers.

Tory tried to adjust his attitude as he showered up, but his thoughts were dominated by Isobel. Even after Rebecca came to pick him up, he found her lovely form and stunning looks couldn't distract him from his misery.

"You're not very good company, you know that?" she chastised him as the waiter brought their drinks. They were at a bar-and-grill, seated beside each other in a corner booth. Tory had uttered all of six or seven words since she picked him up and while he desperately wanted to let the matter go, he knew she deserved an explanation.

"I wasn't completely honest earlier, Rebecca," he said, pausing to gauge her response. She didn't look surprised.

"I figured, by the way you've been acting," she said, stirring her sweet tea. "Of course, if you don't want to talk about it, you don't have to."

Tory sighed. He really didn't want to talk about it, but he had no choice, especially if there was to be a future between them.

"My ex-wife...," Tory began, the words like a knife to his heart. Even now, he still wasn't being honest, "Isobel came back yesterday. I haven't seen her in four years and then out of the blue, she just showed up."

Rebecca continued stirring, though it was clear her drink was agitated enough.

"It brought up a lot of stuff I thought I dealt with a long time ago."

Another lie.

"What did she want?" Rebecca asked, her voice flat, monotone.

"Help," he said simply.

She nodded.

"And did you help her?"

He still was...

"Yeah."

She smiled.

"You're a good man, Tory Jamison. But I really hope this attitude isn't how you intend to deal with all this 'stuff'. It's not becoming of you."

He had to give her credit for her honesty.

"I hadn't intended on dealing with them like that, no," he replied, with a sigh.

"That's good, because I like you better when you're the sweet, caring man I met in the ER," Rebecca said, releasing her straw and looking up at him with a smile. Tory couldn't help but smile back and without thinking, he leaned into her and kissed her on the lips. Rebecca was caught by surprise, but it didn't take her long to respond. She kissed him back, and for a moment, Tory was free of Isobel and all the 'stuff' he hadn't dealt with. He pulled back from her and licked his lips. She tasted like strawberries and tea.

"Let's skip dinner. I feel like dessert," he said, in a quiet voice.

Rebecca smiled, her lips an inch from his.

"Let's eat dinner and then we can get to dessert later, alright?" she whispered.

Tory smiled back.

AFTER THEY finished eating, Rebecca took him down to the lake for a walk around the park.

"This is your idea of a date?" he asked, somewhat out of breath as they walked down the nature trail.

Rebecca took his hand and pulled him along.

"Come on, a strong guy like you, fretting over a short walk?"

Tory didn't mind her teasing him, and he certainly didn't care that she still held his hand as they continued walking. She had a strong grip, but her hand was soft, and he liked the way it felt.

"I want to show you something," she said, smiling again.

They walked hand-in-hand for about half a mile before they came to a wooded area. Rebecca veered off the path and led him to a clearing in front of the lake. The water lapped onto the shore as a cool breeze blew by them. She pulled him over to a clear patch and sat down on the ground. Tory looked at the lake dubiously and then back at Rebecca.

"Just watch," she instructed, and turned back to the water.

He followed her gaze to the sun as it dipped lower into the horizon. A myriad of colors—purples, pinks and oranges—painted the evening sky as night descended upon them, their reflection mirrored in the water. The scene was beautiful.

"I found this spot when I was on a call not too long ago. Isn't it just beautiful?" she asked, her sights still focused on the scenery in front of them. Her eyes lit up as she spoke.

"It certainly is," he agreed, watching her. Deciding it was time to continue what they started in the restaurant, he leaned into her again and kissed her. Taking her face between his hands he deepened the kiss, running his tongue along her bottom lip. She opened her mouth and invited him in. Tory thought of nothing else except how good she tasted. He was happy to be lost in the moment and pulled her closer to him. She rested her hands on his shoulders and seemed to melt in his embrace.

Tory withdrew from her lips to leave a trail of kisses down her neck. Rebecca groaned. He could do this all night.

"Want to go back to my place?" he managed to ask between kisses.

He normally didn't move this fast in his relationships, but given everything that had occurred in the past day with...

"Uh huh," came her response, distracting him from his thoughts.

Neither moved to leave, though. He continued kissing her neck, moving slowly back up to her mouth and down the other side of her neck.

"We should go," Rebecca stated, without much conviction.

Tory mumbled his agreement, leaving kisses on her collarbone.

She pulled back.

"We should go," she stated again, her voice low and enticing. Her face was illuminated by the moon's light, and Tory had to readjust himself when he saw her lick her lips. "We should go now."

She gave him a quick kiss on the lips and stood up. He followed after her and the two walked quickly back to her car. Tory could see how flushed her face was and he was pleased to think that he was one who inspired that reaction.

The drive wasn't long, but it seemed to drag out as he thought about getting her back to his place to enjoy more of her. They had known each other for a while now, and while this was technically their first date, Tory knew it was time to take their relationship to the next level.

Rebecca glanced at him as she drove, smiling brightly. He didn't have to ask what she was thinking; he could see it in her eyes. She pulled into his apartment complex and parked her car. Tory exited the car and walked around to her side. She opened her door, so he couldn't be a complete gentleman, but he took her by the hand and shut the door after her. He kissed her on the lips and then pulled her back towards his apartment. He kept his eyes on her as they walked hand-in-hand.

Then she stopped quite abruptly, her smile gone. Tory followed her gaze to the bench outside his apartment, brightly lit by the streetlight above it—where Isobel sat.

Dammit! he thought, along with a slew of other expletives. How could he forget she was still there?

Isobel averted her eyes and in a quiet, timid voice, said, "I was locked out."

As if that qualified as an apology.

Rebecca pulled her hand out of his and quietly uttered, "Why don't I just call you another time?"

Tory opened his mouth to argue, but what was he going to say? *Come in anyway, just ignore my wife?*

Without looking back at him, Rebecca turned around and walked to her car. She started the engine and left, while he beheld Isobel, who didn't even have the decency to look penitent. She was ruining his life again and all she could do was look down at her lap?

Tory walked by her and went inside. He didn't even bother waiting on Isobel as he made his way to his room and slammed the door shut.

Four

ISOBEL NEVER CONSIDERED HER-
self a religious person, but there was
something about losing everything that
made her drop to her knees in search of
purpose. Given the fact that it was Sunday, it
was only fitting she go to church. She sat in
the back, in case someone recognized her and
started asking questions. And while she had
every intention of paying attention, she
found her mind wandering.

What was she going to do now? Where
would she start? Was there someone she
knew who could possibly take her in? She had
no intention of staying with Tory beyond the
two-weeks and she didn't want to rely on
Pastor Martin longer than she had to. She
could apply for assistance, but it was not her
intention to stay in the area. Still, if that's
what it took to get back on her feet, then that's
what she would do.

Halfway through the sermon Isobel
looked up to see Pastor Martin making eye
contact with her. He paused briefly from his
sermon and smiled at her before continuing.
She blushed to be the center of attention and
slid into her seat, wishing she could
disappear.

Before the service ended, she slipped out and headed home. She took her time, knowing Tory would likely be his unpleasant self. She had left before he awoke again so she wouldn't be in his way. Now, though, as she walked back to his apartment, she wondered if that was so wise. Though his car was parked in the lot, the front door was locked. She knocked a couple of times but there was no answer. She was locked out.

Isobel sighed and walked over to the bench. She noted the time. Five-thirty. Certainly, he would be home soon...right? She sat back and remembered the day she moved in. It wasn't anything special— certainly her apartment was bigger than his— but it was the significance of it. She was *Mrs.* Tory Jamison. Isobel couldn't help but smile at the thought. There seemed to be so much hope that day.

Hope. It was an alien concept, but there was something about the familiarity of her circumstance that made her hope again. Maybe it was being in this apartment, or being around Tory again; whatever it was, she felt like she could put the past behind her and move forward into a future where she was someone again.

Isobel waited for a couple of hours before she heard a car pull up. She sat up, waiting to see Tory turn the corner. Her heart dropped though, when she saw him with a tall, beautiful blonde who seemed to be in love with him. Worse than that, he seemed to be in love with her. Tears welled up in her eyes as her face flushed.

The woman stopped and Tory regarded her at that moment. She could see his expression change from joy to anger. She averted her gaze and quietly offered, "I was locked out," as an excuse. She could feel her face burn with embarrassment. Was he really bringing a woman there while she was staying with him? Did he forget she was there? Was he trying to run her off? God, why didn't she just keep going? Why did she have to come back here to see this?

Isobel heard the woman say something and then turn back the way she came. Tory didn't move and Isobel didn't look up. She didn't want to see his expression, nor did she want him to see her red face.

Finally, Tory stormed by her and went inside. Isobel didn't move. Why did Pastor Martin insist on her staying with Tory? She had told him she'd rather not, but it was either that or the street. And while sleeping on a park bench was not something she wanted to do again, it was preferable to seeing Tory with another woman—and not just any woman, but a tall Amazon who was beautiful, blonde, perfect and could have easily been a swimsuit model. Of course, Tory would be with her. She was nothing like Isobel, who was short, overweight, and dull in appearance.

You should just leave. Obviously, he's happier without you.

Rather than go inside, Isobel heeded the quiet voice and walked back towards the bus stop. She was going to find Pastor Martin and ask him if there was anywhere else she could go. He put her in this mess, and he could fix it.

And what if he can't?

Well, she would figure it out later.

After an hour on the bus routes, Isobel made it back to the church. There were only a handful of cars in the parking lot and it started to rain. She banged on the door, hoping and praying Pastor Martin was there. As the rain came down harder Isobel knocked on the door again, resigning herself to the fact that her life sucked and this was just confirmation of it.

The door opened. An older woman Isobel recognized as the pastor's wife stood there.

"Is Pastor Martin still here?" Isobel asked, holding her hood over her head, though she was already wet and cold. She could only imagine what she looked like. "Please. I know it's late, but I really need to talk to him," she pleaded.

The woman opened the door wider and ushered her in.

"Oh, my dear, you're soaked. I'll get him and bring you a towel. Wait here, okay?"

Isobel nodded, shivering.

The pastor arrived within minutes, followed by the woman, who held a sheet in her hands.

"Isobel," Pastor Martin asked her. "What's wrong?"

But Isobel did not respond. Instead she eyed the woman as she walked over to her and laid the sheet on her shoulders.

"It's not much but it's dry," she offered.

"Thank you," Isobel managed to say.

Pastor Martin led her to his office. Isobel sat down in the chair across from him, holding the sheet tightly around her without making eye contact.

"Now, are you going to tell me what happened?" he asked as he sat back in his chair.

Isobel took a deep breath. She had planned what she would say, but now that she was facing Pastor Martin, she didn't know how to start. Her mouth was open and her eyes on the man, but words failed her.

"How is Tory taking you being back?" he asked.

She shrugged her shoulders.

"Angry. Indifferent."

Pastor Martin nodded his head in understanding, and though Isobel loved the man like the father she never had, his patience and even-keeled manner annoyed her to no end.

"Have you talked to him?"

She shook her head.

"He doesn't want to talk to me. He doesn't want an apology. He just wants me gone. I...I can't be there." She could feel her skin flush. "He brought a woman over." Pastor Martin arched an eyebrow but didn't say anything. "I mean, he came home with another woman. She didn't stay once she saw me, and Tory just went inside, but he didn't say anything, and I could tell he was mad. I can't stay there, Pastor. I can't."

Again, he didn't say anything, making Isobel feel terribly uncomfortable. She saw the sympathy in his eyes, but there was something else, something knowing that unnerved her and made her want to go somewhere else and forget everything.

"What are you running from, Isobel?"

"I'm not running," she insisted. "I just don't belong there anymore."

He shook his head.

"If it hadn't been this, then it would have been something else. You're running Isobel, and you've got to stop."

Anger rose up in her.

"Why are you so insistent I stay?"

"Every time something doesn't go according to your expectations, you go. School didn't pan out, so you left. Marriage wasn't what you expected, so you left. Job after job after job, because you couldn't deal with the idiosyncrasies of your coworkers. How long are you going to do this? How long are you going to keep running? You are a beautiful, intelligent, young woman. You are capable of so much more than this, but only if you stay and plant yourself."

Isobel looked away from Pastor Martin, still angry. Her eyes stung with unshed tears and as much as she wanted to keep them that way, she knew she would be crying shortly.

"I just…want my life back. But I can't do that here…," Isobel muttered; and though she was loathe to admit it, she added, "Tory doesn't love me anymore; I thought maybe since he hadn't filed for a divorce it would be okay to stay, but he hates me. And he's got someone else. I don't want to see him with someone else."

"Then where will you go? I told you I won't have space for a couple of weeks. There's another women's shelter but they're just as full as we are." He paused, waiting for a response. When she gave none, he continued, "No, the situation is not ideal, but you have a bed, a roof over your head, and you have a friend. Here. In me. And in Tory. I don't know how serious he is with this young lady, but I know he's just trying to deal with you being back. Give him time."

One tear finally broke through. Then another. Isobel couldn't deny them anymore than she could deny the truth. Pastor Martin was right; all she ever did was run away from her problems, never staying long enough to face them.

"Isobel?"

"What if I can't?"

"Can't what?"

"Change. What if I can't change? I've been running for so long it's all I know how to do."

He looked at her thoughtfully and asked, "Do you want to change? Do you want to settle down?"

She nodded.

"Then remain faithful."

She stopped crying and gazed at the minister, perplexed.

"What do you mean? Like in a relationship?"

"Not quite. Have you ever read the book of Hosea?"

She shook her head.

"Oh, then I'm sure you'll like the story. There was a woman, Gomer. A nice girl. Pretty thing. Marries a young man named Hosea. He's an up-and-coming man-of-God. A real catch, her father tells her as he walks her down the aisle, but something in her can't reconcile the fact that she's from the wrong side of the tracks. It's a match made to fail.

"But she goes through with it anyway and within a year's time, she gives birth to their first child. Hosea is proud of the family God has blessed him with, but she is not happy. She wants something more, something else, and starts looking for that something in the arms of another man. And then another. And then another. She gives birth to a second and third child, not knowing who the daddies are. In time, Gomer leaves to find what she can't find at home.

"Eventually, she hooks up with a man, a sturdy, handsome fellow. But he's not good to her; he doesn't love her or cherish her like Hosea did. To him, she's nothing more than a warm body, and because her life isn't bad enough, she can't leave this guy because she's indebted to him.

"One day, Gomer sees Hosea in the market. Their eyes meet and for a split second, they are inundated with the love they once knew. Just as quickly though, they must turn back to their respective worlds.

"Well one evening, not too long after, there is a knock on her door. It's Hosea, come to get her back. He pays off her debt and without a word, takes her home. She is nervous, frightened of what he would do to her. But as they enter the house they once called home, he turns to her and simply says, 'be faithful'."

Pastor Martin paused briefly, as he sat back in his chair.

"Isobel, there is more to life than living, just as there is more to marriage than sex. When Hosea told her to be faithful, he meant not just to him, but to herself as well. He meant it for every aspect of her life. Be faithful to who you were created to be. Be faithful to who you want to be—who you, Isobel, want to be. You came back for a reason. There's a part of you that knows there's a better life out there than the one you've been living. But you're not going to find it by running from who you are. You're not going to find it in the past. You've got to look forward. Gomer couldn't find contentment because she couldn't see herself as worthy of love, but she was, to Hosea and to God. And now I'm telling you the same. You are worthy. You are a child of God. Stay and remain faithful to that knowledge and that hope."

Isobel dropped her gaze, unable to respond, unable to look him in the eye, unable to see the hope he spoke so confidently of.

"Will you stay?" he asked. "Put up with Tory for a couple more weeks? We'll talk to Ms. Nancy Syas about signing you up for the jobs program. She's the director there. She's a wonderful person, got great rapport with the women. What do you say? Will you stay?"

Five

TORY WOKE UP TIRED. HE HAD barely slept since Isobel's arrival and though he wasn't usually a negative person, he knew he wouldn't be getting any sleep until she left. He got up and dragged himself to the bathroom. Recalling the events of the previous day, he knocked on the bathroom door first. There was no response. He entered, did his business, and went to the kitchen for some coffee. It was still early, but part of him expected Isobel to be up and cooking breakfast. She had always been a morning person. Today though, the kitchen was dark and empty, just like it had been before she came back.

Shrugging off that thought—or was it wishful thinking?—Tory got ready for the day. Before he left, he slapped an extra key on the counter for Isobel. He didn't want to find her on the bench again waiting for him. The thought made him angry, as he remembered how Rebecca's voice changed and her body stiffened at the sight of Isobel. He would have to smooth things over by telling Rebecca the whole truth this time, and then begging for her forgiveness. It would work out though.

He had no doubts that they would soon be finishing what they started.

This particular thought made him smile. Rebecca was a pleasant person to be around and he needed that.

In a better mood now than when he woke up, Tory grabbed his helmet, his bag, and his bike, and rode over to the clinic. Unfortunately, he couldn't find a moment's peace there. Charlie Dyer, a physician's assistant who worked at the clinic with him, hounded him all day about his date with Rebecca, and though Tory did his best to avoid him, he just couldn't.

Tory left his office and walked back to the nurses' bay in the hallway. He was talking with Janice about calling in a different prescription for Hannah, whose first cream caused an additional rash, when Stephanie approached him, a grim expression on her face. She was one of the nurses who worked the front desk and normally had only smiles for him. He grew concerned.

"There's an officer here to see you," she said, quietly.

His first thought was that it was Rebecca come to see him, but surely Stephanie wouldn't have been so dour if that was the case. Was this about one of his patients then?

Perhaps it was about his parents. Had something happened to them?

"I took him to your office, thinking you were back there," she added.

He thanked her and braced himself for possible bad news as he walked back to his office. As he entered, he spied a tall man with broad shoulders in a sports jacket waiting on him. He took a deep breath and introduced himself.

"Doctor Jamison," he said. He stuck out his hand; the police officer returned the gesture and they shook.

"Detective Harris," he said, offering Tory his badge to inspect. Tory looked at it long enough to note the man was from out-of-town.

Tory released Harris' hand and walked over to his desk. He motioned for the man to sit down and asked, "How can I help you?"

The detective sat upright and maintained eye contact with him.

"I'm looking for this woman"—he leaned forward and slid a photo across the desk to him— "and I'm hoping you can help me find her."

Tory was relieved this had nothing to do with his patients or his parents. He extended his hand to grasp the photo, when he saw who the woman was.

Isobel.

He drew his hand back and sat back without touching it. Actually, he melted into his seat, as though trying to move as far away from the photo as possible.

"What's this about?" he asked.

"She's wanted for questioning."

As much as he wanted to take his eyes off the picture, Tory couldn't. Isobel was smiling in the photo. Try as he might, Tory couldn't remember her smiling like that when she was with him. Perhaps when they were first married, but everything seemed to go downhill from there. He was finishing his residency at the time and worked a lot, so he wasn't there for her as he should have been. But Isobel wasn't exactly trying to make their marriage work either. There were fights about money, and other things, though he couldn't recall what exactly. And then there was her tendency to shut down and threaten to leave. Tory couldn't remember how many times she made that threat. Then one day she left. He was hurt, but he wasn't surprised. Isobel wasn't happy, and there was nothing he could do to make her so.

Apparently though, someone else did and it was a terrible blow to his ego to see that. Deep down inside, part of Tory wanted to know where she had been, what she had done, how she ended up where she was now, but he didn't want to know who or what he had been replaced with.

"Doctor Jamison," Harris said, bringing him out of his thoughts. "Have you seen this woman?"

Tory cleared his throat.

"Can I ask what she did? Or allegedly did?" Not that it was in him to defend her; Tory simply understood how the process worked.

The policeman looked back at him, as though trying to decide if he could trust Tory or not. Finally, he said, "She's wanted for questioning in the assault of an officer."

Tory cringed. Of all the trouble she had to get into...

"I understand she was your wife, but it's imperative we talk to her," Harris stated, "She needs to own up to what she did."

Something in the way the man spoke left Tory feeling uneasy. The detective was taking the situation personally; and maybe he had a right to—Tory didn't know the details and to be honest, the more he thought about it, the more he didn't really want to know. He didn't want to be mixed-up in whatever trouble Isobel was in. And if this officer had traveled out of state to find her and bring her back, then it had to be serious.

Tory was having trouble believing Isobel could assault anyone though. She wasn't the type of person who fought—she was a runner. She took flight when a situation got bad. Hell, it's what she did to him. And no, he couldn't say he knew her now as well as he did four years ago, but none of this sounded right.

Still, he had to say something to this detective who had traveled so far to find her. If he admitted the truth now to a man whom he didn't know and had no reason to trust, Isobel would be gone out of his life, probably forever. He wasn't sure that was good. Not like this. But if he didn't acknowledge Isobel was back, then he was the one in trouble. Maybe he could talk to Rebecca, see if she could get information on this.

If she would just return my call…

"She left four years ago," Tory replied, finally able to tear himself away from her image. "I haven't seen her."

Detective Harris took the photo and placed it back in his breast pocket.

"If she does contact you, be sure to call me," he said, handing him a business card.

Tory said nothing as the man left, his eyes fixed on the card: Detective David Harris. Homicide. This was not good.

Charlie stuck his head inside the door then walked in. Tory groaned as the man sat down in the seat the officer had vacated. Judging by the smug look on his face, Charlie had heard the conversation.

"This whole thing makes sense now," he said.

"Just stay out of my business," Tory retorted.

"Kinda hard to do that when you make everyone a part of it with your attitude. Really, Tory, you wear your emotions on your sleeve, and you've been a miserable S.O.B. since she came back," Charlie said, kicking his feet up on the desk. There was some humor in his voice, but Tory knew he wasn't joking.

"I don't remember asking your opinion about it," Tory said as he placed the card in his wallet, so he could remember to talk to Rebecca about it.

"Well, as your friend, I'm offering it to you, free-of-charge. Send her packing. You don't owe her anything." All the humor was now gone from his voice.

Tory shrugged him off.

"Friend or not, this is my business and I don't need your input, thanks," he said.

"What about Rebecca? How does she feel about having to share you with your psycho ex-wife?"

He shook his head.

"Isobel's not psycho," he responded, though he didn't know why he was defending her.

Charlie stood up, shaking his head.

"You know what she did…"

Tory turned to him, indignant.

"Yes, and I don't need you reminding me. Butt out and let me handle this."

Charlie threw his hands up.

"Just remember you put yourself in this position," he stated as he walked out of the office. "Don't say I didn't warn you."

Tory sank back into his seat and sighed. He understood Charlie's concern, but why couldn't the man respect his decision? He wasn't doing this for Isobel, he was doing this for Pastor Martin, and it was just for a couple of weeks. Less than a couple of weeks now. She would leave again and that would be it. This was his good deed for the century and then he could get back to his life—to his miserable, lonely life.

TORY WAS glad to leave work after enduring Charlie's self-satisfied attitude for the remainder of the day. His plan was to go home and watch a basketball game. Maybe he would grab some burgers or something, then call Rebecca again. He had left a couple of messages for her when it became clear she was avoiding him the same way he was avoiding everyone else. He could do nothing else though until she called him back.

With a tired sigh, Tory strapped his bag to his back, put his helmet on, and was on his way home. He focused on traffic and getting home safely, finding his mood lighter and more agreeable as he rode into the complex. He even waved at his neighbors, who were outside playing with their children. Tory got off his bike and walked it into the tiny foyer of his apartment.

Before he shut the door, the aroma hit him. Lasagna. His mouth watered as the blend of garlic, tomatoes, and cheese enveloped him. He couldn't remember the last time he had lasagna.

Yes, he could. It was right before Isobel left.

He removed his helmet and set his bike by the door. Isobel was in the kitchen pulling the garlic bread out of the oven and setting it on the counter beside the lasagna. He was puzzled to think he had all this hiding in the cabinet. Certainly, Isobel had picked up the items necessary to create such a meal. He admitted he wasn't good when it came to keeping up with his household; that had always been Isobel's job. After she left, it didn't make sense for him to buy groceries regularly. He got what he needed when he needed it and if he was hungry, which was hardly the case these past few days, he simply went out for what he had a taste for. Granted none of it was healthy, but it kept him going.

Isobel looked up at him then. He didn't know why, or maybe he did, but in spite of all she was doing for him—the cooking and the cleaning—he couldn't see beyond the fact that she left him. He became annoyed almost immediately and walked by her without a word. He took his bag to his room and changed out of his scrubs. He wanted to relax, watch the basketball game, and forget the world around him. No more phone calls. No more questions. No Isobel. Just him and his television.

He walked back out into the living room. Isobel was still in the kitchen, right across from space he called his living room. With her there, he couldn't remember why he thought the apartment was comfortable. It seemed so crowded now.

Tory dropped on the couch and put his feet up on the cushion, trying to ignore the smell of dinner. He wasn't hungry, and he wasn't going to eat her food, he told himself as he reached behind the pillow for the remote. It wasn't there though. Nor was it on the floor. Or on the pillow behind his head. In fact, nothing was where it normally was—it was all *clean* now.

"Where's the damn remote?" he growled at Isobel as he stood up and turned in her direction.

Isobel stopped what she was doing and though she didn't look directly at him, she pointed to the coffee table. He looked down and there it was, the television remote, right in front of the television. Tory snatched it up, upset. Yes, it was in a logical place, but she shouldn't have touched it to begin with.

"Just leave my stuff alone," he grumbled as he dropped back down on the couch and started flipping through the channels. He found the game, but he couldn't concentrate: Isobel was putting away dishes and making noise. He turned the volume up and tried to focus as a player went for a three-point shot.

Then Isobel dropped a pot on the counter. Tory looked up at the clatter and missed the shot. Angry, he gritted his teeth together and clutched the remote so tightly his knuckles turned white. Why couldn't she just let him enjoy the game in peace and quiet?

Isobel cleared her throat, but he didn't bother turning around.

"I made a plate for you," she said, her voice still low.

Why doesn't she just speak up? Not that he was going to answer her. Tory kept his eye on the television as she took her plate back to her room. His stomach growled. He briefly considered getting the plate she made for him, but he was determined—he wasn't going to take anything she had to give. If she thought she could come back and earn his favor, his forgiveness, by cooking a mouth-watering, sense-delighting, made-from-scratch, home-cooked meal...

Tory's stomach growled again.

No, he wasn't going to give in.

His stomach argued, reminding him that he had barely eaten today because he was too busy avoiding Charlie.

Tory sighed and stood up. The plate Isobel made for him was right there on the counter waiting for him, holding as much food as he could eat. The pasta was covered with meat and so much melted, gooey cheese, he started salivating. He groaned. He really wanted to eat, but he couldn't just accept the meal. That would mean he was accepting her, and he was not going to do that.

What if he just tasted it? That would satisfy his desire, wouldn't it? Just a taste?

Tory picked up the fork Isobel left for him and cut a small piece off the corner. A string of cheese followed him as he raised the fork to his mouth. The food was hot, but delicious. He remembered the first time Isobel made it for him and smiled. She had insisted on cooking for him for their first date. Her grandfather had been a chef for a five-star restaurant and taught her the recipe for it, along with many other meals. They spent the night eating and sitting on the couch next to each other, their bodies intimately close, but not in a sexual way. Oh, the attraction was very obvious, but there was something about just being with her that made him feel complete.

Just as quickly as the smile came though, so it faded as he thought about the hurt and the pain she brought him afterward. He hated to focus so much on it, but he couldn't reconcile the fact that she didn't deserve his forgiveness. She didn't deserve anything but his anger and contempt.

Tory put his fork down. He wasn't going to eat.

Again, his stomach argued, and he began rationalizing.

If I made my own plate, then I wouldn't be accepting what she made for me. After all, I am letting her stay free of charge for two weeks. This is the least she can do.

Content with his decision, Tory grabbed a clean plate—a plate Isobel had cleaned—and scooped up a big slice of the lasagna and large hunk of the garlic bread. He sat back down on the couch and was able to enjoy the game in between bites of food. He was eating far too quickly to savor the tomatoes and the seasoned meat, but he was enjoying it nonetheless. He even went back for seconds, saying nothing when Isobel came back into the kitchen to clean up. She put away the leftovers and washed the dishes, saying nothing about the plate he left behind.

Six

ISOBEL SIGHED AS SHE CLEANED up the leftovers. Tory had made his own plate, leaving the one she fixed for him nearly untouched on the counter. He just needed time, Pastor Martin had said, and though she returned only with the intent of getting temporary help from her former pastor, she now found herself yearning for Tory's forgiveness. Based on the way he was acting though, there was no way she was going to get it.

Still, she had to stay and endure the consequences of her actions—something she wasn't in the habit of doing. Running away was programmed into her DNA: her father left when she was eight and her mother was gone by the time she was fourteen. She stayed with her stepfather for a couple of years before she too flew the coop following her grandfather's death.

Isobel was tired of running though. She didn't want to be that person anymore, even as she grappled with the words Pastor Martin challenged her with and fought the urge to dump Tory's dishes in the sink. Instinct mandated she grab her bag and go, but she knew she had to stay; she had more than herself to think about this time. She was going to be a mother, and if she could get her act together then maybe she could even be a better mom than hers was. The woman was a miserable human being with a sharp tongue and a negative disposition who often looked for reasons to put everyone down. It had been fifteen years since Isobel last saw her, but she didn't miss her. Still, there was no denial as to whose daughter she was based on the traits she exhibited, and Isobel hated herself for it. But if she wanted to change, then she had to stay. No, the situation wasn't ideal, but it was a start: a new baby, a new life, and a new Isobel.

Too bad the new life didn't come with a partner. Tory hated her and David...

Isobel looked ruefully at the dish water in front of her. Even if Tory hated her, being in the same room with him was better than being with David. She loathed to think that she had left a man like Tory for someone like David, who showed no qualms about hitting and debasing her.

Of course, he was nothing like that when they met. He was a handsome man, with short, light brown, almost blonde hair and flashing, blue eyes. He had a tall, commanding presence with broad shoulders and a solid frame. And he was charming too. She didn't know why his love should be any better than Tory's, but when he offered it, she readily accepted and moved in with him. And she was happy for a time. In her mind, life was how it should've been—except it wasn't. He changed, or rather she did, little-by-little as time pressed on. The first time he hit her, she left. But then he apologized, promised never to hit her again, and begged her to come home. She did and that was the end of the matter. Until he hit her again. And again. And again. Though she thought about leaving, she stayed because she convinced herself she had nowhere to go. She had alienated everyone because of him. And besides that, he was a cop. No one would believe a man who had sworn to uphold the law would break it. So, she was stuck, enduring the beatings, the abuse, the anger because she couldn't leave.

Isobel considered the irony of the situation: she left Tory but stayed with David. She chuckled out loud, before realizing Tory was still in the living room. She turned to see he was still focused on his game, then went back to washing the dishes.

Maybe she stayed because she felt she deserved what she was getting, but when she found out she was pregnant, she vowed her child would not be subjected to that pain. She had yet to tell David about her pregnancy, trying to find a way to give him the ultimatum: the beatings stopped, or she was gone. She knew in her heart she didn't love David but if he was willing to change, she was ready to make the situation work. Unfortunately, it didn't happen that way.

Isobel couldn't recall what the argument was about; all she remembered was his fist slamming into her back. The hit knocked the breath out of her, and she fell over. She stayed down, knowing what would come next. Kick after kick until her back and legs were bruised. It wasn't the first time she had taken a beating, but as she lay on the floor in pain, she swore it would be the last.

While he yelled at her she looked around the room. She needed an opportunity, a weapon, something to fight back with.

"I work hard to provide for you," he spewed at her.

She saw nothing but an empty, glass vase sitting on the table beside her.

He grabbed hold of her hair and pulled her up. He was volatile, ready to erupt, but he seemed to want to control himself, to show remorse for what he had done. With his free hand, David cupped her face and looked intently into her eyes.

"Don't you understand how much I love you?" he asked her.

Isobel held back tears. Her back hurt, her legs shook, and her head was pounding. She didn't how much more she could take. She had to do something. Her hands free, Isobel felt her way towards the vase. David was too distracted to notice. Her fingers barely grasped the glass as he pleaded with her.

"I don't want to hurt you."

Isobel reached out further, wrapping her fingers around the container. David noticed then what she was trying to do, but it was too late. She lifted it up and slammed it as hard as she could against him. It didn't have the impact she wanted, but he dropped her. Unfortunately, he was incensed now. He took a moment to recover, then turned back towards her, his eyes red with fury.

She gathered herself and hit him once more with the vase, shattering its glass body. He threw his arms up to protect himself and didn't suffer any injury. Then he reached out and hit her again. She fell to the floor. He tried grabbing her, but she crawled away from him, her heart was beating so loud she couldn't hear herself think. He pulled on her ankles. Isobel tried kicking him, but he wouldn't let go. As he dragged her over the glass, Isobel grabbed onto a large piece, gripping it hard. She ignored the pain in her hand as the shard cut deep; and when he turned her around, she raked the piece across his neck, drawing blood.

The cut was deep enough to stop him. David let go of her and grabbed his wound. His eyes grew wide with shock and he sat back, staring bewildered at the blood that covered his hands. He was too stunned to fight back—for the moment.

Isobel wasted no time. She grabbed her coat and her purse and left. That was two weeks ago. She used what little money she had to pay for a motel room for a few nights, but when the funds for that ran out, she was stuck. Isobel couldn't stay in the area: she had to assume David had gotten medical assistance and was searching for her. She could go somewhere else, run away and start her life again. But she was pregnant now. And scared like she had never been before. Though it was a risk to return to the familiarity of her former life, one she never talked about with David, Isobel did so anyway and prayed she was free of David.

Tory came up behind Isobel. She jerked as he placed his plate on the counter and then walked away, leaving her to finish his dishes. Part of her was glad he had at least accepted what she cooked, even if he ignored her and was rude to her. The other part of her? She wasn't sure yet, but at least she didn't have to worry about Tory hitting her as David did.

A WEEK passed, and this became their routine: Isobel made herself useful, while Tory ignored her. She cleaned, did his laundry—anything to garner his favor—but he only responded with indifference and as few words as possible.

While Tory was at work, Isobel met with Ms. Nancy at the church. She was an older, cheerful woman, who smiled all of the time. As Pastor Martin promised, she was more than happy to help Isobel plan her future. Isobel was reticent at first, not wanting to explain her situation with David, but she found an understanding soul with Nancy.

"The past is in the past. The important thing now is your future and what you will do to get there," the woman reminded her.

Nancy helped her with her resume and signed her up for some basic job skills and interview workshops. And with that, Isobel experienced hope for the first time in a long while. She even began to ponder whether she should stay or not. When she came to Pastor Martin looking for help, she never intended to settle, but after being away from true friendships and love, Isobel couldn't see moving on away from him and Nancy. It did her heart good to know there were people out there who cared for her and maybe she was being selfish, but she wanted to feel loved.

Unfortunately, this wasn't something she could say of Tory's parents, her in-laws. That's what they still were, after all, though Isobel wasn't sure if they knew it. Henry and Sarah Jamison showed concern when Tory initially brought her home, but in the years that followed, they grew to accept her. At least Henry did. Like any other mother, Sarah had reservations and she had no problem sharing them with Tory—then and now.

"'Tory, this is your mother. I've called you twice now; you haven't answered either of your phones and you haven't called me back. Mrs. Cooper said she saw Isobel at church on Sunday. Is this true? Call me.'"

That was the first message. Others followed quickly followed:

"'Tory, why aren't you answering your phones? I've tried you at work. You need to call me back.'"

"'Tory, this is your mother, again. I'm not playing games with you. Call me.'"

"'What is this I hear about Isobel staying with you? After what that woman did? You need to call me.'"

Isobel cringed when she heard the last message play. Tory was unaffected though. He simply ignored it, and Isobel, until it was time to eat.

Seven

TORY SUCCESSFULLY EVADED his mother for six days, but he knew that wouldn't last. It was simply a matter of time before she finally caught him. And he wasn't being pessimistic; he just wasn't the lucky sort. After all, Charlie was still being curt, and Rebecca had yet to call him back. He had called her several times, but each time he got her voicemail.

"You've reached Officer Rebecca Garner. If you are experiencing an emergency, please dial 9-1-1. Otherwise, please leave a message and I will return your phone call as soon as possible."

"Rebecca, please. It's Tory. I just want to explain. Call me, okay?"

And because he couldn't think of anything else to say that he hadn't said already, he hung up. Maybe he had screwed things up, but all he needed was one chance, one opportunity to explain everything and fix the situation. *Dear God*, he sighed, *can I please just have one thing go right in my life?*

His phone rang. He let out a sigh of relief, certain God had answered his prayer.

"Why haven't you called me back, Tory Edward Jamison? I have been calling you for days now."

It was his mother.

Dammit. Out of the frying pan and into the fire.

"And don't even think about hanging up. I'm not above going down to that clinic where my only child is concerned."

Tory loved his parents and often humored his mom when it came to her protectiveness over him, but this was one of those times he wished he had siblings so he could deflect the attention she was giving him.

He cleared his throat.

"Hi Mom."

"Don't get smart with me. Just answer my question."

"What? I just said hi."

"You've had a week to say hi. Why haven't you called me back?"

"I've been busy here at the clinic. You know we're open on Saturdays and I often sleep on Sundays."

The statement was true…*enough.*

"What is this I hear about Isobel being back?"

And so, it begins. Tory rubbed his temple. He could feel a headache forming.

"You shouldn't believe everything you hear." He was going to pay for this, but if she left him alone even for a little while, it was worth it.

"Mrs. Cooper said she saw Isobel at church on Sunday. And Mrs. Cooper is not like those other busy bodies who have nothing better to do than gossip. So, is she back? Was that her at church?"

Damn Isobel. She never went to church before. Why did she have to start now?

Well, that's just the wrong attitude to have, isn't it? he thought to himself. He should be glad she was looking for some form of salvation.

Not when it means I get harassed by my mother.

"I didn't go, so I can't verify that."

"And why didn't you go?"

I was out drinking.

"I had a late night Saturday."

"Hmm!" his mother grunted.

"Look, I'm a grown man—"

"So, you're telling me that Isobel hasn't contacted you?" she interrupted him. "Or that she's not staying with you? Because if she is—"

"Ma, enough!" he exclaimed, realizing too late that he not only interrupted, but yelled at her. He felt like he was a child again, about to get in trouble. But he wasn't a child, and his life was just that: his. He didn't have to explain himself to his mother, his friends, or to anyone else.

"I just don't want to see you get hurt again," his mom declared with a sniffle, though he knew it was as true as his lies. "I can't help it that I worry about you. I'm your mother. You'll see one day, when you have kids."

He sighed.

"I know, and I appreciate it, but I am capable of taking care of myself."

His mother remained silent. Tory wasn't sure if this was a good thing or not, but he was going to take advantage of it.

"Listen, I've gotta get going," Tory said quickly, then added, "Tell Dad I love him, and I'll talk to you later." Then he hung up. His actions would certainly not sit well with her, but he was not discussing his life with her. Not right now. And really, not ever.

THE END of the day came, but Tory lingered. He spent a little bit more time with his last patient, filled out more paperwork, and found reasons to stay at the clinic. He didn't want to go home. There was nothing waiting for him there.

"What are you still doing here?" Melissa, one of the nurses, asked him. She was usually amongst the last to leave.

"I'm getting ready to leave, actually," he lied, but he could see she didn't believe him. With a hand on her hip, she asked, "Who are you trying to fool?"

He shook his head. As much as he didn't want to be bothered, he did appreciate her concern.

"Apparently, not you," he replied.

"Come on, then," she said, waving him out of the office. "Walk me to my car."

Tory obeyed. He didn't say much as he packed up his bag and grabbed his helmet. It was dark outside, but he never minded riding his bike at night; he just had to be more attentive to his surroundings.

Melissa talked about her daughter and grandson as they walked to her car. Tory barely listened, though he nodded at regular intervals. He just couldn't focus.

"You are not very good company," Melissa said as they reached her car.

"I'm sorry," he sighed. "I was just lost in my thoughts."

She smiled and simply stated, "Everything eventually works itself out, darling. Just hang in there long enough." She had been at the clinic for as long as he had, and knew some of his history, but she never prodded or nosed her way into his business. Tory appreciated that—then and now.

"Thanks, Melissa."

"Goodnight, Dr. Jamison," she said, getting in her car. "Be safe getting home."

He nodded, but he wasn't going home—not yet at least. He mounted his bike and rode it until he was tired and winded. He rode past his apartment and into downtown. The city was lit up and alive with people of all ages and types enjoying the evening with dinner and libations. His stomach growled, and he realized he had barely eaten again today. He looked around for somewhere to stop, a place that was quick, where he wouldn't need to be social.

His regular pub. At least he had one consistency in his life.

Tory got off his bike and walked it down the main street, looking at the neon lights around him. He secured his bike to a tree and made his way to the bar entrance. He walked past the business folks standing around the door and found an empty table. A server came by with a menu. After ordering, Tory sat back and waited.

"Dr. Jamison."

Tory looked up at the mention of his name. It was Pastor Martin.

"What are you doing here?" he asked, curtly.

"Getting dinner," he responded with the usual smile on his face. "Mind if I join you?"

Tory raised an eyebrow. This was the last person he wanted to share a table with.

"If I say yes, will you still sit down?"

Feigning offense, Pastor Martin placed a hand on his chest and let his mouth drop open.

"I'm hurt," he said.

Tory shook his head.

"No, you're not," he argued.

"You're right, I'm not."

The cleric pulled out a chair and took a seat as the server came back with Tory's drink. He set the beer in front of him and turned to Pastor Martin.

"What can I get you?"

"I'll just have whatever he ordered."

When the waiter left, Tory remarked, "You sure are trusting. You don't know what I ordered."

"Nope. But when you've been around as long as I have and seen the things I've seen, you learn to read people; and right now, I'd say you look like the burger and French fries type."

The young doctor shook his head in annoyance.

The minister shrugged and sat back.

"So, how're things going with Isobel?" he asked.

Tory narrowed his eyes and shot Pastor Martin an unappreciative glare.

"What?" the minister asked, innocently.

"I know what you're doing, and you can just stop now."

"What am I doing?"

"You hoped by me taking her in, I'd forget all the hell she put me through, magically fall in love with her again, and we would live happily ever after."

Of this he was sure: his pastor was playing cupid. Tory couldn't help but picture the man with a bow and arrow, running around shooting unsuspecting victims—like himself—with arrows of love, the same man who was drinking beer with him, had tattoos up and down his arms, and still let out a swear word every now and again when he got mad enough.

Pastor Martin didn't argue though, just gazed at him, an expression of sadness on his face.

"She's changed, you know," he finally said.

Tory sighed.

"I know." He was still trying to figure out if it was good or bad, but yes, he knew.

"Apparently I've changed too. Everyone keeps telling me I'm bad company."

Though this was not something he could deny. He *was* bad company; he had a big 'ole attitude and he was okay with it.

"It's not wrong to hurt, Tory. But you can't continue acting like this."

"Why not?" he snapped, "It's your fault I'm even in this situation. My life wouldn't be so complicated now if you hadn't brought her back."

"You're the one who said yes," Pastor Martin calmly reminded him.

"You didn't leave me much room to argue."

"You are a grown man. I simply put it in front of you."

Tory groaned with disgust. Pastor Martin was the only person to acknowledge his volition in this matter. Unfortunately, it was for Isobel staying.

"Do you still love her?" the minister asked.

Tory refused to answer. Of course, he didn't.

"Look, I have a whole lot of advice— good stuff too—but it only works if you're willing to talk to me."

Tory shook his head.

"You know as well as I do that your attitude is just as important as your action. If you haven't forgiven her, then this can be a starting place for you. Regardless of whatever you think my motives are, you said yes, and I suspect you did it because part of you is ready to let the past go."

Tory didn't look at the cleric, just down at his beer, as one tear slid down his face. He wiped it away quickly and cleared his throat, hoping to play it off.

"Do you want to forgive her?" Pastor Martin asked him.

Tory couldn't stop the next tear from falling, nor the one after that. They were long overdue and if he was completely honest, it was about time he dealt with them.

"How...," he asked, his eyes still on the beer, "Do I do that?"

"Speak tenderly to her," the minister said simply.

Tory looked up and glared at the man. This was the good advice he had to offer?

"That's it?"

Pastor Martin sat up and leaned into the table, towards Tory. He met his gaze and replied, "In this situation, yes."

"You're not going to admonish me to pray or read the Bible?"

"Obviously, prayer and reading your Bible helps, but if you want to start on the path towards forgiveness, begin speaking tenderly to Isobel. Have you ever read the book of Hosea in the Bible?"

Tory shook his head. Pastor Martin smiled and sat back.

"Oh, it's a great book, a romance actually, and I know guys don't read romances as a rule, but it's a meaty story with sex, betrayal, and a happily-ever-after. The whole package deal. A man, Hosea, fell in love with a girl from the wrong side of the tracks. Gomer was her name and she was a gorgeous young thing. She could make your heart stop beating with a bat of her eyelashes. They got married and lived happily ever after.

"Well, that's how the story should have ended, but it never does, does it? They did the marriage thing, went out with other couples, had a baby or three, but there was just something in Gomer that couldn't be satisfied. Hosea loved her and tried to overlook her faults, but when rumors started flying around about her fidelity, he couldn't ignore it anymore. He confronted her about it, and she confirmed his fears: she was being unfaithful. Well, he tried reasoning with her, begging her to be faithful, trying to get her to love him, but in the end, she just left, abandoning her children to him.

"One day, years later, he ran into Gomer in the marketplace. She had gotten mixed-up with some guy she owed money to and was now repaying her debt by warming his bed. Their time apart should have deadened their hearts to any emotion still lingering within them, but when their eyes met, it was like they were smitten teenagers again, strolling in the park, talking until dusk, lost in each other's presence.

"They returned to their respective worlds, but Hosea couldn't get her out of his mind. All night, he wrestled with his emotions, until he heard God tell him to speak tenderly to her. You see, if he could be kind to her, treat her with decency, remember what their love was, then he could begin to see her as someone worth cherishing, someone to be taken care of, someone to be forgiven."

The minister stopped talking and looked to Tory for a reaction. Tory just sat quietly though, digesting the tale. He understood what the man was trying to say but suggesting that someone forgive and actually doing it were two different things. How was he supposed to speak tenderly to Isobel when he didn't know how to act around her; much less, when he couldn't stand to be in the same room with her? He'd admit his attitude was the biggest problem, but was this really the solution?

"So," he said, unable to think of any other response, "What happened to them?"

"Hosea paid her debts, took her home, and worked things out."

"And everyone lived happily ever after, huh?" Tory said sarcastically.

"Who doesn't love a happy ending?" Pastor Martin replied.

"And this is what you think I'll do with Isobel? Live happily ever after?"

"What can I say? I'm a romantic at heart. Plus, you two are still married."

After Isobel left, Tory hoped beyond hope she would return, but she never did. Heartsick turned to bitterness, and then numbness, as Tory did all he could to forget Isobel. And forget her he did, until she showed up at his doorstep. Maybe he should have cut ties and dealt with the end of his marriage sooner.

"It's a mistake I intend to correct," Tory retorted, then added, "Besides, I'm seeing someone and am quite happy with her."

Or I would be, if she would just call me back...

"And you should be, Tory. You don't have to work things out with Isobel if that's what you choose, but until you forgive her, you won't be able to move forward. You'll be stuck on this treadmill you're on, walking miles at a time, but getting nowhere. Just speak tenderly to her. View her through the words you speak over her and see if you're still able to hold onto your resentment."

Eight

BECAUSE ISOBEL HAD EXPERIENCE in office administration, Nancy was more than happy to put her to work helping her. She asked Isobel to file several weeks' worth of paperwork who completed the work in no time.

"You are so diligent in your tasks," Nancy gushed.

"You're too kind," Isobel remarked with a smile, pleased with the compliment.

"You can never be too kind," Nancy said. "That's like saying you can shop too long or eat too much chocolate. There's no such thing."

Isobel laughed.

"So, what's next?" she asked, as Nancy sat down in her chair.

The older woman looked around her desk and settled her sight on a tall stack of papers.

"Can you sort these for me? They're the rules and regulations for the new residents. It's about nine pages, but I forgot to hit the collate button on the copier," she explained.

"Sure," Isobel said, walking around the desk to grab the stack. The office wasn't very big; cozy was a better description, but Isobel was okay with that. She appreciated the company that came with the small quarters, especially since Tory was still giving her the silent treatment. Not that it mattered anymore. Within a week she would be moving on, and while the mission was not the most ideal living space, at least she wouldn't have to deal with him.

"…Isobel…"

Isobel looked up and realized the other woman had been talking to her.

"I'm sorry," she said, sheepishly. "What were you saying?"

"Don't be sorry, I was just gabbing," Nancy remarked. "Anyway, the hole-puncher is over in that cabinet. When you get to a stopping point, we can go get some lunch. I think we have a new chef today in the kitchen," she said as she looked back to the files in front of her.

Isobel also returned to her work, but she couldn't concentrate; her mind raced with thoughts of her future and her child. She knew she had a lot to consider, but first she had to start with the basics, which meant taking care of herself so that her baby could be healthy, but she needed help with this. Isobel felt like a leech asking for help, but She had no choice.

She cleared her throat.

"Can I ask you something?" she asked.

"Of course, dear."

"Do you have any kids?"

Nancy looked up, not at her but the ceiling.

"Biologically, I have three. One boy, two girls. They're in their twenties. My son is probably about your age. Then I have two stepsons, both in their thirties. And an adopted girl. She's my baby at sixteen."

Isobel stopped working to listen. Six kids?

"Wow," she said. *And I'm fretting over one*, she thought to herself.

"Tell me about it. Just think—I had a house full of teenagers for about a decade. It was enough to make a grown man cry. Or at least hide. There were days my husband seemingly disappeared. I'd find him in our bedroom or the bathroom, hiding from them."

Isobel chuckled.

"Even still, they are my greatest joy."

It was heartwarming to hear her say so. At least something positive could come out of their situation.

"What's on your mind?" Nancy asked her.

"Well...I am. I just..." She sighed, then started again. "I'm pregnant."

Nancy smiled, walked over to Isobel and wrapped her arms around her.

Isobel was unsure of how to react.

The older woman pulled away and looked at her.

"Regardless of the circumstances, a new life is always something to be celebrated."

Isobel nodded, tears stinging her eyes. She wasn't sure why she wanted to cry, but ever since she got pregnant, it seemed she could tear up at the drop of a hat—the other circumstances in her life notwithstanding.

"How far along are you?" Nancy asked.

"About two months, I think."

"Have you been to a doctor yet?"

"No."

"Well, we'll have to see about that," Nancy said, and talked about getting her assistance so that she could see a doctor; about how they worked with the doctors at the clinic; and how they would get her settled before the baby came. She continued talking. To see Nancy so excited made Isobel feel loved.

Then she mentioned Pastor Martin. Isobel straightened up and interrupted.

"No," she said. "You can't tell him."

Nancy was surprised.

"Why not? He'll be happy for you."

"I know, but I don't want him to tell Tory."

Nancy quietly gazed at her until she felt uncomfortable. Isobel turned away and finished explaining.

"I'm only with him for another week. There's no reason to make him more upset."

"Well, if that's what you want, I'll respect it, but I will say you need as much support as you can get right now."

"Maybe, but Tory wouldn't take it well. I don't want to chance him finding out."

"He might surprise you," Nancy said with a smile. She reminded Isobel of Pastor Martin for a moment, the hopeful spirit he perpetually exhibited reflecting in her eyes.

"I don't know. He's been everything but understanding. I just don't see how he'd accept this. I don't even know how to talk to him anymore."

Nancy placed her arm around Isobel's shoulder.

"That comes with time, my dear. Don't push it, just let it happen. There is nothing you'll be able to say that Tory won't come to see for himself. You'll see."

"I wish I had your optimism."

"Oh well, that too comes with time."

ISOBEL ARRIVED home later than usual. She preferred to get there before Tory to minimize her contact with him. Today, though, he actually beat her home.

Curse public transportation, she thought. The actual trip to the church was only twenty minutes, but, on the bus, it was one hour and six minutes, plus the ten minutes it took to walk to the stop.

She took a deep breath and braced herself for Tory's less than congenial attitude toward her.

That's not what she got though.

Tory was in the kitchen emptying grocery bags. This was her first surprise. The second one came when he looked up and made purposeful eye contact with her. Her eyes widened, and she couldn't help but wonder what was wrong with him. He seemed nervous and his lips were twitching as though he wanted to say something. It was a little nerve-wrecking. After a few wordless moments of this, Tory finally cleared his throat.

"I ah...I picked up groceries today," he said, handling a package of rice. "I was wondering..." He paused, struggling to speak. "I was wondering if you would mind fixing your dirty rice tonight," he continued quickly, then pointed to the food. "I think I got everything."

With her eyes, Isobel followed his hand down to the counter and though the items were meager by most standards, he had gotten the necessary ingredients for the meal.

Why is he being nice though? She thought he was kind of lean, though in a good way. Did he miss her cooking? Judging by the contents of his cupboards and refrigerator, the answer to that was probably yes, but it didn't explain why he was acting the way he was. He had no problem eating the food she had prepared for the past week. He had no problem letting her use the little money she had left, not once asking her about it. And now he was not just buying groceries, but also asking her to cook?

Why are you questioning his attitude change? she chastised herself. Hadn't Pastor said all he needed was time? Maybe Tory was finally getting to the point where he could forgive her. If she could help expedite the process with a pot of dirty rice, then that's what she was going to do.

"I can do that," Isobel said.

He offered her half a smile, which was better than no smile at all, and awkwardly pointed towards his bedroom. He was still wearing his scrubs and she knew he would want to change.

She nodded and put down her bag to get started.

An hour later, the rice was ready, prepared with a side of peas and rolls. Her grandfather had taught her how to cook before he died. Truth be told though; she never appreciated the talent she had for it. She didn't mind cooking for Tory in the beginning, when their love was new, but when it became a requirement, when it was something he expected and didn't seem to appreciate, she grew to despise it, especially there at the end, before she left. But now, as she prepared the food, knowing it was something Tory missed, she actually enjoyed doing it.

Isobel set out two plates as Tory's phone rang. His face lit up as he recognized the caller and he answered it with enthusiasm.

"Rebecca!"

So that's her name, Isobel thought as she returned to the sink. She picked up the skillet and slowly ran the sponge over it so that she could listen.

"I'm so glad you called back," Tory continued, his back to her.

Isobel's heart sank. She would be lying if she said she wasn't jealous; but it seemed strange that she should feel this way now. She had left him without a thought to whom he might be hooking up with. Why should she care now?

"I know...I know...," Tory said and started towards his bedroom. Isobel didn't look his way as she continued to wash the dishes, seemingly oblivious to his conversation. Most of it was indistinct, but some words were as clear as day:

My ex-wife...my minister...two weeks...only a favor...leaving in a few days...want to continue what we started...really enjoy being with you...

Isobel was done listening after that. She ran the hot water to rinse the dishes and made as much noise as possible to drown out his voice. She could tell by his tone that he was enamored with this woman. All of a sudden Isobel felt the urge to bolt, to grab her bag and walk out the front door, to put Tory behind her, the way he obviously did her.

Isobel shut the water off and dried her hands. She turned around and looked at her purse, which she had left near the door. She could just leave. Slip out while Tory was talking to his girlfriend. He wouldn't know, and even if he did, he wouldn't miss her. Yes, he seemed willing to be nice to her earlier, but he was too infatuated with this other woman to pay Isobel any mind.

Just pack your bags and go. Throw all your things into your backpack, leave what doesn't fit, just like last time. There is nothing here you need...

But you promised you would be faithful.

Tory doesn't want you here. All you're doing is just messing up his life again.

But he let you stay. That was his decision.

But if I wasn't here...

Do you want your child to run like you did?

Isobel stopped arguing with herself. If she left now, she would only be perpetuating the cycle: she would eventually walk out on her child, abandon it, just like her mother abandoned her, and then her kid would run away, just like she did.

No more running, she told herself. No matter how much she wanted to go. No matter how painful it was to face Tory knowing he was happy with someone else. Knowing she had screwed things up again. Just a few more days and Pastor Martin would have a place for her. Then she could live her life and Tory could live his...without her.

Taking a deep breath, Isobel picked up one of the plates, a spoon, and a glass of water, and walked back to her room. Her hands trembled the whole way, but she was determined to remain steadfast in her decision. She would just have to be sure to steer clear of Tory.

Nine

TORY WAS HAPPY TO HEAR Rebecca's voice. What was more, she actually seemed glad to hear his.

"I'm sorry, I've just been slammed at work. You know how it is," she said sweetly. "But you do owe me an explanation."

"I know. I know," Tory agreed, walking back to his bedroom, keenly aware that he had an audience. He closed his door, sat down on his bed and explained everything. He told her about Isobel, though he did not mention the fact that they were still married—an oversight he was going to change. He told her about Pastor Martin and doing him a favor, told her about the two weeks, and lastly, told her about wanting to see her again.

"Slow down, Dr. Jamison," Rebecca said. "Three is a crowd and I don't want to get in the middle of your 'situation'."

"I told you, she'll be gone by week's end. There's no situation."

"I don't know," she replied hesitantly.

Tory waited for her to finish her thought. He wanted to see her again and hoped he hadn't ruined his chances with her.

"It just seems perhaps with everything that happened," she continued, "Maybe you're not ready for another relationship."

Before he could stop himself, Tory moaned.

"Oh, not you too." It seemed no one could see that he was just reacting to the events of the last week. Why were they reading into it? "Listen, Rebecca, I really enjoy being with you. Isn't that enough?"

"Everyone's got baggage. I'm not knocking you for that. I'm just suggesting maybe you haven't adequately dealt with yours and pursuing something with me at this point would only complicate things."

Tory couldn't understand. None of this would have been an issue had Isobel not returned. Granted, his life was complicated now with his soon-to-be ex-wife living with him, but that problem was going to be remedied in days. Surely, she could see that.

"Are you going to talk to me or just sit there breathing?" she teased.

"Breathing is working just fine for me right now," he responded, tongue-in-cheek, though he couldn't hide his disappointment.

"I really enjoy being with you too, Tory. I just don't want to get hurt, that's all."

"I wouldn't hurt you," he assured her.

"Not intentionally, but if what you say is true, then I'd rather take this slow. Can we do that?"

He offered her a smile, though he knew she couldn't see it.

"We can do that," he said.

With that settled, they talked for a while longer before Rebecca advised him she had to go. Tory promised he would call her again the next day and she said she'd like that. His heart skipped. Maybe this would work itself out too.

He hung up and looked at his phone. He couldn't think of a single thing wrong with his life. Except that he was hungry.

Tory made his way back to the kitchen where he found a plate of rice waiting for him. He warmed it up and sat down in front of the television to eat. He went back for seconds and when he had his fill, sat back down to watch the game. His team lost, but he was okay with that. Rebecca had called, and they were okay.

He dropped his plate in the sink and started to the bathroom when it occurred to him that his kitchen was clean.

Because Isobel cleaned it after making the dinner you requested.

It was the least she could do, came one very bitter voice.

Speak tenderly to her, came another.

Great, he thought. He was carrying on a conversation with himself like it was the most natural thing in the world, and not just today. Tory fought Pastor Martin's advice for days. It was a nice story and all, but speak tenderly to Isobel? The same woman who left him after promising him forever? And just what the hell did that even mean? Isn't that what got him in trouble in the first place?

Still, the more he thought about the advice, the more he knew he couldn't ignore it. Did speaking tenderly mean warm, affectionate feelings? Or was it just plain human decency? Had it been anyone but Isobel, his mother would have been appalled by the way he was treating her and would have quickly chastised him.

"I taught you better than that, boy," she would have said with a smack to his head.

The fact was Isobel had changed; whatever she went through had humbled her. And it wasn't as if she came back looking for him either—she just came back. She had even apologized. Sort of. She was certainly apologetic, which was more than she had been in the past. She had changed for sure.

While he was making himself miserable.

Okay fine, so Pastor Martin's advice was good, just as he said. Where did he start, though? Because when he saw her, all he could think about was what she did. What was it Pastor Martin said?

"If he could remember what their love was, then he could begin to see her as someone worth cherishing. Someone to be taken care of. Someone to be forgiven."

Tory had to admit her company wasn't all that bad. She did help him. She did what she used to do, without the fussing, of course. He chuckled as he recalled how his habits annoyed her to no end. Like the laundry. How often did they have to rewash his clothes, or God forbid, her clothes, because he forgot to finish what he began? It was a little endearing, thinking about the colors her face made when she discovered her good underwear had been sitting wet in the washer for a day. It was then he would take her in his arms and kiss her plump, juicy lips.

But she left, came that voice.

I have to start somewhere, he told himself. He wasn't ready to offer his forgiveness, but he could offer a friendly word.

Except every time he saw her, he didn't know what to say. He argued with himself and chose to avoid her just so he didn't appear to be completely crazy. Finally, he settled on the one thing he knew for certain about her— her cooking. Admittedly, he took it for granted while she was with him, but now that she was back, he realized how much he missed it. Certainly, this was a safe-enough topic to speak 'tenderly' about.

So, with his words planned out, Tory purchased groceries, ashamed to think he had allowed her to do that for him given her current situation and waited for her to come home. He had trouble meeting her gaze and the words seemed to stick in his throat, but when he said them, when he asked her to cook, he found they weren't as vile or bitter as he thought they would be. It was strange, but for the first time in days, he was able to see her as the Isobel he married.

Tory returned to the kitchen, picked up his plate, rinsed it off, and placed it in the dishwasher. He shut off the lights, did his business in the bathroom, and softly approached Isobel's room, determined to offer a 'thank you'. If there were no other tender words to be spoken tonight, it would be those.

The light was on in Isobel's room, but Tory didn't hear anything.

She's gone to bed. Just let it drop. You've said enough already, came that voice again, inspiring Tory to do the exact opposite. He knocked on the door and waited. If she was asleep then fine, he tried, but he wasn't giving up. He started to knock again, when he barely heard, "Come in."

Her voice, it seemed, had become permanently low.

He opened the door and saw that she was in bed. She sat up, her eyes nervously moving between him and the wall to his left.

Speak tenderly to her. Remember she's someone worth cherishing. Someone to be taken care of. Someone to be forgiven.

"I just wanted to say...," he said, his own voice as low as hers. Her eyes settled on his, something between confusion and hurt filling them. He didn't understand it, but he didn't feel like dragging this out any further. He wanted to acknowledge what she had done and go to bed. "Thank you. For making dinner."

She looked to the wall again and said, "You're welcome."

A very unpleasant silence followed. Tory looked around the room. He hadn't given it much thought when she came to stay with him, but he used this room as a storage closet. He was surprised she found the bed. It wasn't bad, now that she cleaned it up as much as possible without throwing stuff out, but he hadn't even given her the compassion worthy of a human being. Tory sighed and looked down. He had enough of the tender speech tonight.

"Well, thanks," he said, unsure of what else to say, and as he shut the door, quickly added, "Good night." He didn't stop to listen to her response, if she had one. He just wanted to go to bed.

Ten

TORY WAS QUITE CONTENT WITH himself when he went to work the next day and despite his best attempt to act normal, he just couldn't.

"Well, look at you, Mr. Sunshine," Stephanie greeted him when he walked in.

He smiled at her, unable to think of a witty response. He was going to have to do better in the future.

"Your favorite patient is here," she added, referring to Hannah.

He looked at his watch.

"This early?" he asked, more to himself. Then he looked at Stephanie suspiciously. "What did she do now?"

She couldn't contain her smile. He noticed Melissa was biting her lip trying not to laugh.

"She stuck a rock up her nose," Stephanie said.

Melissa burst out laughing.

Tory shook his head. Of all the things Hannah had done, this one topped them all. He dropped his bag in his office, grabbed his stethoscope, and was met by Janice in the hallway.

"Miss Hannah is waiting for you in Room 3," she said, as apathetic as usual. He knew she cried, evidenced by Hannah's 'treatment' of her last time; he wondered though, if she laughed. Even he couldn't hide his amusement. He grabbed her chart, eying Janice for some hint of emotion. She walked away without a bat of her eye.

Maybe she didn't.

In Room 3, Hannah was opening all the cabinets and drawers, a broad smile on her face. Her mother, Ashley, sat in a chair wearing a tired look on her face.

He took a seat on the stool Hannah rolled over to him and said, "Thank you."

Hannah giggled and went back over to the cabinet. Tory watched her for a moment, amused by the fact that she was her usual self. If it wasn't for Ashley's worn presence, he would have sworn there was nothing wrong with her.

"So, you just came to see how I was doing, right?" he asked.

Ashley rolled her eyes.

"I swear, she does this stuff just to watch me bug out."

Tory laughed.

"What happened?" he asked.

"I don't know. We were outside just for a minute, a minute, before I put her in her car seat. Hadn't gone a mile down the road when she complained that the rock in her nose hurt. I almost put the car in a ditch. I went back home to see if I could get it out, but it must be stuck up here"—she pointed to the bridge of her nose—"so I called here and after Melissa finished laughing, she told me to come in."

He placed an understanding hand on her shoulder, though he couldn't help the smile.

"Alright, Missy," he said, turning to Hannah. She stopped opening and closing the drawers and looked at him. "Can I take a look at your nose?"

He learned a long time ago that Hannah was not partial to having anything done to her that she didn't want done. If he had her cooperation, like her booster shots over a week earlier, then things went smoothly, and she made seasoned nurses like Janice cry. A win-win situation.

Hannah glared at him for a moment, before she replied, "No," and turned back to the drawer.

Okay then, he thought, as Ashley stood up.

"Hannah, Dr. Jamison wants to see the rock in your nose. Can you show him?"

Hannah looked up, appearing to think about it.

"No."

Ashley threw Tory a tired look and went over to pick up her daughter, who suddenly realized she was about to be ambushed. She tried to slip around Ashley, only to bump into Tory, who picked her up. She tried to squirm out of his embrace, but he held on.

"Hey, let's make a deal, okay?" he said to her. She perked up and looked at him with interest. "Let me see the rock in your nose *and* get it out, and I'll give you a cool sticker. What do you say?"

Hannah didn't look amused.

"No."

Tory sighed, but he wasn't ready to give up.

"How about a very cool sticker and a lollipop?"

She took a deep breath and said, "Okay." She went limp in his arms and let him sit her down on the examination table.

Bribery. He'd have to remember that should he ever have children.

With Ashley's assistance to keep her still, Tory pulled out a pocket flashlight and peeked up her nose. Sure enough, there was a small pebble stuck in the bridge of her nose. He couldn't dislodge it though.

"I see it," he announced, as he stood up and turned to Ashley. "It's wedged in there really good. I'll have to get the forceps to get the rock out, but we'll need to hold her down."

"Okay," she acquiesced. "Maybe if it's bad enough, she won't do this ever again."

"That's the spirit," he said encouragingly, and patted Hannah on the shoulder. "You be a good girl, let me get the rock out and I'll give you two very, very cool stickers."

She raised her eyebrows.

"And two lollipops?"

He shook his head.

"Do you just come see me for lollipops?"

She giggled and nodded her head.

Tory smiled back.

"Okay, let me get Janice and I'll be back."

He went back out to the nurses' bay, only to find Janice laughing. She straightened out when she saw him and asked, "Did you get the rock out?"

"Not yet," he said, "But you're going to help me."

Janice said nothing and between the two of them, the rock was extracted within minutes. Tory gave the little girl two very, very cool stickers as promised. She quickly took the backings off of those, stuck them to her face and happily awaited her lollipops. She was in for a rude surprise when Tory gave the suckers to Ashley.

"She'll give them to you, okay?"

Hannah scowled and crossed her arms in front of her. She tightened her lips and refused to even look at him.

"I guess I don't get a 'thank you'," Tory said.

"I'll say it then," Ashley said, putting them in her pocket. "Thank you."

"Anytime," he responded, sincerely.

THE REMAINDER of Tory's day was comparatively quiet. He dealt with the usual—colds, physicals, rashes, and fevers—but his mind kept going back to Hannah. He found himself wanting to brag on her. Even when they had the forceps in her nose, she didn't scream or fight as much as other children he had seen. He was proud of the way she handled herself, never mind that she had put herself in that situation in the first place.

Tory was still in a good mood when he got home and found Isobel in the kitchen cooking dinner. His mood threatened to sour, but in the time Isobel looked up and then back down, Tory decided he didn't want to spend his evening miserable. His day had been too good for it to end like that. He offered her a quick greeting, though it sounded more like a grunt, and walked back to his bedroom to change. A smile crept onto his face as he thought about Hannah. Like before, he wanted to brag on little girl and share his day with someone, but Rebecca was working the late shift this evening. He wasn't going to call his mom; by now she would have figured out he lied to her. If he talked to his dad, then there was a hundred percent chance Tory would end up talking to his mom. Yes, it was inevitable, but he preferred to put it off as long as possible. He was just lucky she hadn't come busting into his home, demanding he put Isobel out.

Isobel. He could talk to her.

But she...

She's here, he finished. *And what's more, she's changed.* It didn't alter the past, but perhaps it could change his future. Perhaps he could forgive her.

With a deep breath, Tory meandered back into the kitchen. Isobel was sautéing onions, peppers and garlic, a divine aroma if there was ever one. He stopped by the counter, ready to talk to her, but nothing came out. Speaking tenderly was not so easy. Maybe he'd give it a minute.

He sat down in front of the television, but he was too fidgety to remain there and wondered if Isobel would listen to him.

Tory got back up and walked back over to the counter behind Isobel. Her dark brown hair was in a messy bun on the back of her head and she was wearing one of the t-shirts she left behind. It fit snugly on her, accenting every curve in her upper body.

He pushed the thought out of his head, only to find one reminding him of her abandonment of him.

Speak tenderly, he told himself, and cleared his throat.

"What are you making?" he finally said.

Isobel raised her head but didn't look at him.

"Jambalaya," she responded in her usual tone. "I'm using the leftover rice."

"Oh," Tory uttered. Certainly, he knew whatever she cooked would be delicious, but he didn't want to talk about that. He just wanted her to listen.

Gathering courage, he walked around the counter to the stove so that he stood beside her. She seemed apprehensive about him being so close to her, but he wasn't going to let that stop him.

"Can I...ah...?" he started as she turned those light-brown, radiant eyes towards him. He almost lost his nerve. Almost. "...tell you about my day?"

Isobel stared at him, as if trying to decipher why he was being so nice.

I guess I would be wondering the same thing, he thought, even while he hoped she wouldn't turn him down.

"Sure," she said.

Tory smiled and told her about Hannah and her mom. He told her about the rock and the nurses. He even told her about Hannah saying, 'thank you' to Janice the last time he saw her. He kept talking as Isobel finished cooking and plated the food, setting out the napkins and spoons.

"She sounds really cute," Isobel said.

"She is," he said, then added, "Though I'm sure there are times Ashley doesn't think so. She certainly didn't think so this morning."

Isobel smiled. Tory noted how it was the first time since she returned that he saw her smile. He forced himself to stop thinking, lest his thoughts stray any further in either direction.

Without making eye contact, she gave him his plate. He looked down at what she handed him, noting how she was, again, taking care of him.

"Thank you, Isobel," he said and was surprised to find his words were sincere.

Eleven

ISOBEL WAS SURPRISED TOO. THIS was the first time Tory acknowledged her and called her by her name. But in that, she found she wanted to cry. The emotion welling up in her was foreign and she didn't know what to make of it; she just knew he was the cause. What was he doing? Was he setting her up?

No, he isn't David.

Then why is he being nice now?

Don't complain, Isobel. Isn't this what you wanted? For him to forgive you? Just let it go, take your plate and go eat, she told herself, as Tory went back to the couch to watch television and eat.

We used to sit together, she thought, then turned abruptly back to her plate, pushing the thought out of her mind. Used to, those were the key words. Those times were gone and there was no way he would ever take her back. Not that it was an option ever. She was just saying...

Oh, dammit! Just be grateful he's treating you decently, she told herself.

With that, Isobel took her food and went back to her room. She had been hungry, but not anymore. Her stomach was churning, and her head was starting to hurt. She lay down on the bed, hoping to settle her stomach, and buried her head under the pillow. Without meaning to, she fell asleep.

NANCY HAD Isobel helping in the kitchen that Friday, where the church ran a cafeteria that fed the mission residents. She didn't mind assisting, whether it was serving or cooking—anything so she didn't think about Tory. She continued to be bothered by the fact that he was being nice to her. It wasn't that she didn't appreciate it or suspected he had ulterior motives, but it was bringing up old feelings she didn't want to explore. There was no way she would be able to just walk away from Tory with her heart intact if she did that.

Isobel grabbed a couple of latex gloves as the female residents lined up against the wall, waiting for the 'lunch bell' to ring. She was going to be serving them today, but she couldn't help but think about how this was going to be her starting next week. She watched them as one of the ministers said grace. Everyone stopped what they were doing to listen. The women were tall and short, black and Latin, skinny and fat. She didn't know the circumstances that brought them there, but she knew she would fit right in.

Her thoughts traveled back to David. Was he looking for her? She hoped not; and given that she had neither seen nor heard from him, Isobel prayed he had decided to let her go. She knew though the truth was entirely different though: David had been possessive of her from day one. He didn't allow her to do anything without knowing where she was going and when she would be back. It didn't take long to alienate the friends she had made. And there was no making new friends. He wanted her all to himself. She started to relax some—only slightly—in the last couple of weeks, but she chose to stay on her toes and be ready for him…just in case.

Isobel looked at the women again as the minister said, "Amen." How many of them came from the same situation she did? How many of them were carrying the scars of their former lives? How many of them left everything behind to start anew? How many of them were still in pain? For Isobel, her bruises had faded, and the pain had long gone; but she knew that was because she had a place to heal at the apartment with Tory. He didn't know about David and the pain she had suffered, but it was enough that he had opened his door to her. She would always be grateful to him for that.

She sighed. Regardless of where her thoughts went, she always ended up thinking about Tory. Well, she was done now. She had a job to do, then she was going to talk to Pastor Martin about staying at the mission so she could say good-bye to Tory—forever.

IT WAS well after five by the time Isobel got off the bus and started her walk towards Tory's apartment. A young woman sat on her front steps talking on the phone as her two young children played in their modest front yard. Isobel waved at the mother, who waved back. She had become familiar with some of the neighbors, many of whom had moved in after she left. They seemed nice enough; like Tory, just hard-working people.

As Isobel came up to Tory's building, she noticed a silver sedan parked in his spot. He drove his car that morning for whatever reason. She wasn't familiar with the all of the folks in his life since she came back. Charlie was probably still a big part of it, he had been Tory's best friend when he started at the hospital. Tory's parents lived in the area, as evidenced by the phone calls. And of course, there was Rebecca. But who owned the car,

Isobel couldn't say. She turned the corner and immediately wished she hadn't.

Tory's mother, Sarah, was sitting on the bench.

She was tall, like Tory, but she was on the heavier side. She reminded Isobel of a candied apple, round up top, sticks for legs. She was dressed professionally and presented herself as a woman with dignity; as well she should since she too was a doctor and conference speaker. She was a hard woman though, and as Sarah's eyes descended upon Isobel, Isobel knew she was about to receive four years of pent-up anger.

Sarah stood up, her full five-foot-ten, two hundred plus pounds adding to her daunting presence. Isobel dropped her gaze and tried to walk past her. She wouldn't admit it then, but she had no problem doing so now: the woman scared her.

"So, you have nothing to say?" Sarah asked, her tone hard and unforgiving.

Isobel stopped. She started to face her mother-in-law, but she couldn't. She knew she didn't deserve forgiveness, but she wished others could at least understand the guilt she lived with.

"Tory's not back," Isobel managed to say.

"No, but I see you are," Sarah responded sarcastically. "And you thought Tory would be the perfect patsy and take you in?"

Isobel wanted to argue, to explain herself, but she knew the woman wouldn't listen. She opened her mouth and stuttered, "I'm sorry." It really wasn't what she intended to say, just what came out.

"You're sorry? That's all you can say, after everything you put my son through?"

Guilt, heaped on like hot coals. Isobel blinked rapidly, hoping to hold the tears back, and turned around. Then she started towards the door.

"Don't you walk away from me, young woman," Sarah threatened.

Isobel pulled the key out of her pocket and fumbled around for a moment, trying to get it into the lock. She heard Sarah walking towards her. Isobel pushed the door open and started to close it, when Sarah put her foot between the door and the frame. As much as she wanted to, Isobel wasn't going to be able to get away from her. Tears broke through and streamed down her face. She left the key in the door, clutched her purse and headed back to her room. Tory's mother followed, calling her name, insisting she stop. But Isobel didn't stop until she had shut the door to her room. She knew it wouldn't stop Sarah, but she hoped.

It didn't. Sarah threw the door open and stormed in. Isobel backed up against the far wall, crying.

"What you do want from me? I said I was sorry."

"And you think that's enough?" she said, taking a couple steps towards her. Isobel knew she wouldn't hurt her, but she couldn't help the fear filling her. It was habit now. "You think you can say you're sorry for the past four years and that will be enough? Do you know the hell you put Tory through? The hell you put us through? I told Tory you would hurt him, I warned him, and you did just that." She pointed an accusing finger at her daughter-in-law.

Isobel hung her head in shame.

"You can act contrite and repentant, but I know you—you're only taking advantage of him because of his good nature. You think you can manipulate him like you did then, but I won't let you do that."

Sarah grabbed Isobel's bag and threw it on the bed. Then she grabbed her wrist and started dragging her over to the bed. Isobel tried pulling her arm back, but she wasn't strong enough.

"You're leaving and you're never going to bother my son again," Sarah demanded.

Isobel saw the intent in her eyes and knew she wouldn't win this battle.

"Mom?"

Both women turned their heads to the door where Tory stood, a look of concern on his face. Isobel wondered if it could be for her.

Not now, she told herself, as Sarah let go of her arm.

"Could've been anyone, huh?" his mother asked him, her hands on her hips.

"This is why I don't tell you anything," he told her; and stepped between them. Isobel was surprised by the move and looked up to him for defense. Sarah's face turned red with anger.

"I am your mother! And you are siding with this no-good tramp?"

Isobel cringed, though it wasn't the worst thing Sarah had ever called her.

"She abandoned you, or do I need to remind you of the misery she left you in?" the woman continued. "You're too good for someone like her."

Even if Isobel had the sense—good or bad—to argue, she would not. She only wanted to sink into the floor and disappear.

Tory glanced at her briefly, his brows furrowed, before he took his mother by the forearm.

"That's enough, Mother," he said and walked her out the door, shutting it behind him.

Isobel didn't move from where she stood, surprised: given the current situation, she hardly expected Tory to defend her like he did.

But he's not defending you, the other voice in the back of her mind argued. He's simply keeping peace. Just like he always did.

Isobel knew the voice was right, especially when she heard Sarah and Tory argue.

"You can't just walk into my place and do that," Tory said, trying to drop his voice.

"I have been calling you for two weeks and you haven't picked up the phone once to call me back. What else was I supposed to do?" his mother responded, her voice loud, her tone offended.

"I am thirty-two years old. I don't need you running my life."

"Apparently you do, if you're letting that woman manipulate you again."

"I'm not doing this with you right now."

"Perhaps then you would like to do this after she leaves you again for the next guy with a bigger dick and bigger paycheck."

"Mom!"

"Oh, stop being so naïve, Tory. What else do you think she's been doing? God only knows what she's contracted in the years she's been away. Or are you sleeping with her already? Is that why you didn't want to call me back?"

"You need to go," Tory retorted, his voice growing more distant with every word.

Isobel sank down onto the bed. Maybe it was selfish of her, but part of her resented Sarah for her intrusion. Everything was going well enough between her and Tory. Why did his mother have to show up and ruin it? Would he revert to his unpleasant, unforgiving self now that his mother had said what she said? Would he find reason to put her out? The two weeks were up, and she hadn't gotten a chance to talk to Pastor Martin. Ms. Nancy simply told her not to worry, but how could she not? She was in limbo, stuck between the past she loathed and a future she couldn't see.

Isobel grabbed her pillow and hugged it tightly to her. She couldn't hear Tory or his mom anymore. Was this it? If he had thrown his mother out, certainly he would have no qualms about putting her out as well. After all, she was the reason he had to do what he did.

She stopped thinking and closed her eyes. She just wanted rest, stability, peace. She wanted...

A knock at the door pulled her out of her thoughts. Isobel took in a deep breath and sat up.

"Come in," she said, though her voice was barely audible.

There was another knock.

Isobel cleared her throat and repeated herself, a little louder this time. Then she braced herself for the worst as the door opened. Tory stood there, looking at her for a split second before averting his gaze elsewhere. She wanted to look away, as she normally did, but she couldn't.

"I...you know...how my mom gets," he stuttered.

She watched him, hands in his pockets, shoulders hunched, eyes on the wall behind her. He looked the way she felt.

Isobel nodded her head in response. And that was the end of it: he turned around, pulling the door shut, as she started to lay her head back down.

But it wasn't. Tory opened the door and turned back to her. Isobel sat up.

"No. She had no right to talk to you like that," he said, making eye contact. "I'm sorry."

Again, this was more than she expected, and she didn't know how to respond beyond a weak nod. He offered her half a smile and turned again to leave.

But like before, he didn't get beyond the door before he turned around again.

"Are you hungry?"

She shook her head.

"I'm okay."

Tory argued though, a soft smile spreading across his face, just the like the one he used to give her when he would try to talk her into something.

"It's dinner-time, I know you've gotta be hungry. Let me take you out to eat. You've been cooking for me for two weeks."

Isobel shook her head again.

"I...I'm okay. I don't want to inconvenience you."

Tory's smile broadened.

"Come on, it's not an inconvenience. What do you say, Issie?"

She stared at Tory, dumbfounded. Did he even realize what he called her? It had been so long since she had heard that nickname uttered by anyone, especially him. Did it mean...?

No, it was nothing more than a slip of the tongue. He wanted to sway her mind and she couldn't say no to him, not when he was smiling at her and calling her Issie.

"Alright," she finally agreed.

"Great," he said, and added, "Let me change and we can go."

Isobel nodded and watched as Tory left to go to his room. She was feeling better after the confrontation with Sarah Jamison, and she couldn't help but smile when she considered how Tory was treating her. But...

"Oh, hell," she said and got up. There was no way she was going to question her situation now. She didn't have to worry about Tory giving her the cold shoulder. She didn't have to worry about being penitent. Tory was going to take her out, so she didn't have to cook, and they were going to enjoy their evening.

Just like they used to.

Twelve

TORY FOUND HE WAS MORE embarrassed than anything else after seeing the way his mother treated Isobel, and as he listened to her put down the woman who was *still* his wife, all he could think about was Pastor Martin's admonition to speak tenderly to Isobel. His mother certainly wasn't, and yes, she had called Isobel far worse throughout the years, but this time he could hear the vitriol behind the words his mother spouted. He certainly understood it, but watching Isobel cower as she did, watching the way she didn't argue back and just accepted the horrible things his mother said, made him ashamed of his own thoughts. Whatever Isobel had done, she did not deserve the indignity of being barraged by hurtful words and this only steeled his resolve to forgive her.

After saying good night to her, Tory went to his room and shut the door. His cell phone rang. It was the church, probably Pastor Martin calling to let him know he had found a bed for Isobel. This was great. It's what he had been waiting two weeks for, what they all wanted, especially him.

So why was his heart beating so hard?

Clearing his throat, Tony answered the phone, but it wasn't the minister.

"This is Nancy Syas, the director of the mission. I apologize for calling late, but Pastor Martin asked me to contact you as he was called to an emergency."

"Is everything okay?"

"Oh, yes. It is now. Just part of his pastoral duties."

Tory nodded, though he knew the woman on the other end couldn't see it.

"Again, he asked me to give you a call regarding Isobel. Unfortunately, we don't have an open bed for her, and I know he promised to update you." She paused and though Tory knew what she was going to ask, he didn't feel annoyed or betrayed. "I know this was unplanned from the start but—"

"She can stay here," he interrupted, finishing without hesitation.

"Are you certain? We don't want to inconvenience you."

"Yeah, it's no problem," he assured her. "She can stay as long as she needs to."

"Thank you so much, Dr. Jamison."

He could hear the smile in her tone.

She told him Pastor Martin would follow-up with him and thanked him again before hanging up. Tory replaced his phone on the dresser, marveling that he was really was okay with Isobel staying with him for a little while longer.

ISOBEL HAD breakfast waiting when Tory got up the next morning. She had always been a morning person, so he wasn't surprised. But he was a little shocked by how she continued to care for him when she didn't have to. It was a truly good way to start the day though, marred only by having to push back negative thoughts about Isobel:

She left.
She abandoned you.
This is the least she can do.
This is all she can do?
She owes you.
Maybe your mother was right.
God knows what she contracted.
She's a whore.

But they weren't as loud as the other ones:

She's changed.
She's repentant.
As bad as I feel, she's carrying the guilt of what she's done...

As a battle of words raged his mind, Tory found himself fighting another conflict: hunger. He inhaled the scent of eggs and pancakes and his stomach growled. All other thoughts were lost. He accepted the cup of coffee Isobel gave him with a "thank you," and sat down on the stool at the counter. Though she moved about getting the food to plates, she kept her head down and avoided eye contact, another reminder of why he should speak tenderly to her.

He cleared his throat and said, "Nancy Syas from the church called last night."

Isobel stopped moving and looked up at him expectantly.

"She said that there were no beds available," he began and paused to take a sip of coffee, unintentionally building the suspense. He watched as her shoulders slumped and her countenance fell. Her eyes scanned his, asking the unspoken question of what she would do now. Well, he would answer that for her. "I told her you could stay here."

Her expression didn't change. She studied his face, perhaps looking for the punchline that ended with 'just joking'. But he wasn't joking. Even after several hours to reconsider his decision—a decision his mother and friends would certainly give him hell about—he knew he was okay with Isobel staying as long as she needed to.

"Are you sure?" she finally asked.

"Yes," he replied and took another sip of the coffee. "You can't really plan ahead when you're in limbo, so just do what you need to do and don't worry about having to leave."

She seemed relieved for a moment, but he wasn't sure. Her expression remained incomprehensible. Finally, she looked down and quietly said, "Thank you."

He smiled, before digging into the plate of food she set before him. It sure beat the cold toast or breakfast bar he usually consumed. He gave no thought to the question that now burned in his mind, *she's planning ahead for her future, so what are you doing for yours?*

AFTER A typical morning at the clinic, Tory went into his office for his lunch break and called Rebecca. She was on duty and couldn't talk long, but she invited him to dinner Friday.

"I thought we were taking things slowly," he teased her, though he was amenable to the idea of seeing her.

"Oh, we are," she said, confidently. "I just don't want to be bored."

"I'll see you then," he said and hung up.

Tory returned to work, ready for Friday to be here. When he walked by the nurses' bay, Janice perked up.

"Oh, you just missed it," she said. He detected a faint smile on her face. "Ashley Meyer called."

Though he was still in a good mood, Tory groaned.

"What did Hannah do now?" he asked.

"She ate some crayons," Janice said, her smile inching higher.

He glared at her for a moment, waiting for her to continue. Surely, she didn't need his advice for this. Crayons were non-toxic for that reason; it was almost a given children would eat them. Still, when he looked at the other nurses behind Janice who were stifling their laughter, he couldn't help but feel he was missing out on something.

"What?"

"Don't you want to know how Ashley knew Hannah ate crayons?"

He sighed. Alright he'd bite.

"How did Ashley know Hannah ate crayons?"

"Her front teeth were red," she said, as the other nurses broke out into laughter. "Her molars were green."

Tory shook his head as he walked off but laughed as well when he was out of their hearing range.

Thankfully the rest of the week went by quickly; as he was looking forward to seeing

Rebecca. He thought about her when he could and didn't even mind when his father called to chastise him for throwing his mother out of his apartment. Tory explained the situation as best he could, knowing his father understood how overly protective his mother was, but in the end, he simply apologized and said he would come over for dinner one night. Not Friday night, though.

With a smile on his face, Tory made his way to Rebecca's townhouse, a bouquet of roses in hand. She lived in a new development on the other side of town. The neighborhood was a good one and the streets were quiet. Several boys were playing football in the street, while a retiree was cutting his grass; this was suburbia at its finest.

Tory knocked on her door. Several seconds later, the door opened and there stood Rebecca.

"He's punctual," she commented with a wry grin on her face. "I like that."

He smiled and handed her the roses.

"And he brought flowers. I like that more," she said, holding them to her nose.

"I am here to please," he stated.

She moved aside so he could enter. Her apartment had a lovely floral scent to it and the walls were a warm, beige color. Tory noted it wasn't much bigger than his apartment, but everything about it was inviting. He followed her into the kitchen and watched as she filled a vase with water.

"Dinner's almost ready," Rebecca stated. "I'm just waiting on the bread."

He inhaled the scent of lasagna and felt his stomach grumble.

"Can I help with anything?"

She shook her head.

"Just keep me company."

"I can do that," he said, taking a seat. They talked as Rebecca began preparing plates. He mentioned his day and asked about hers. When she finished her task, she set their plates on the table. "Bon appetit," she added with a smile.

"Everything looks great," he said.

The first bite was anything but, though. The noodles were rubbery, the sauce was runny, and the meat tasted overly seasoned. It was nothing like Isobel's lasagna. Tory had to fight to keep the food in his mouth, especially when he saw Rebecca watching him.

"How is it?" she asked.

Tory smiled and nodded. Then he grabbed some water when she turned away and quickly washed down the food.

"I was a little worried. I cook little things for myself, but never a big meal like this," she said, sticking her fork into her salad.

I should have started with the salad, he thought. He felt bad, since she tried so hard, but this obviously wasn't her specialty. Not everyone could cook. Some people were more gifted at it, like Isobel. She was a natural... which reminded him.

"Can I ask a favor?" he asked, glad to put his fork down. "I don't want to get you into trouble, so if you can't, don't be afraid to say no. I'll understand."

"What's that?"

Tory reached into his wallet and pulled out the business card Detective Harris had given him. He handed it to Rebecca and picked up the garlic bread, certain there was no way she could have messed that up.

"He stopped by my office asking about Isobel. I didn't feel comfortable enough to tell him anything. There was just something about him...I don't know. Anyway, I wondered if you could check into his story and whatnot."

Rebecca's smile disappeared as she took the card. She looked at it for a minute before responding.

"What did he want with your ex-wife?"

Tory noticed how forced her words were. He watched her, thinking perhaps it was a mistake bringing it up, but this was a simple request. There was something about the guy he didn't trust and now that he lied about Isobel, he was just as culpable as she was. Surely Rebecca could see he wasn't asking on behalf of Isobel, but himself.

"He said she was wanted for questioning in the assault of an officer."

Rebecca cringed.

"I know it's not your business and I hope you don't think I'm asking for Isobel," he assured her. "I just want to be sure everything is on the up-and-up."

She nodded her understanding, though she didn't look at him; she studied the card.

Tory took a bite of the bread. It was very garlicky, but otherwise edible.

"I can look into it," she finally said, "but what happens if she is guilty?"

Tory stopped chewing and looked at her. He hadn't considered that option. He was so focused on forgiving Isobel, he never thought there might be consequences to deal with. Of course, she wasn't his responsibility anymore, so it really shouldn't matter.

"I don't know," he admitted. "I haven't thought that far ahead. Just kinda taking it moment-by-moment."

Rebecca nodded again, but this time she looked up at him. Her expression had changed, but he wasn't sure what to make of it. She put the card down beside her and picked up her fork. She moved her salad around but didn't eat.

Tory didn't know what to say so he took another bite of the bread. So much garlic. He was going to have to gargle several times with mouthwash if he was going to kiss Rebecca tonight. He certainly wouldn't be getting near people any time soon. And he didn't have to worry about vampires.

"So," Rebecca began, stabbing at a grape tomato, "Your ex-wife has moved on?"

"Not quite," Tory said. "They didn't have room for her at the mission, so I told them she could stay until something opened up." He reached for another piece of bread and dipped it in the sauce. He moved the lasagna around and picked at the cheese on top. "This is good, Rebecca," he lied, hoping to lift her spirit.

Her solemn expression didn't change too much as she informed him, "There's more in the kitchen."

Tory sighed and turned back to his food. He managed to finish half of it before excusing himself to the bathroom. He rinsed out his mouth. Twice. The taste lingered—

and not in a good way. He would have to make sure they went out to a restaurant next time.

When he exited the bathroom, Tory found Rebecca clearing out the table. She gave him a soft smile and walked to the kitchen, a plate in each hand. He grabbed a glass and the basket of bread and followed her. He came up behind her and pressed his body to hers as he deposited the items in the sink. He took in her scent: cucumbers and spice. It was a light, airy scent that tickled his lungs as he inhaled. Tory placed his hands on her hips and kissed the nape of her neck, relishing the warmth of her body and the taste of her skin. He let his hands roam up and down her sides, peppering her shoulder with kisses. The sensual act sent tingles down his spine and straight to his groin. There was a connection between them, he thought, something that started the night Isobel interrupted them; well, maybe not interrupted, but definitely stopped, if only by means of her presence.

Wanting more, he turned her around. As he leaned into her to kiss her again though, her hands flew up to his chest. She pushed against him; her touch gentle but hardly intimate. Tory straightened up. Had he misread her?

Rebecca smoothed his shirt, her gaze solid on her hands.

"I hate to call it a night, but I've got the early shift."

It took a moment for the words to sink in.

"Oh," he managed to say, disappointed.

She met his gaze, the side of her mouth turned up, almost apologetically. But she said nothing else. The situation turned awkward quickly.

Tory dropped his arms to his side, then reconsidered and pushed his hands into his jeans. He wanted to take her in his arms, to hold her and touch her as he had been doing, but this wasn't going to happen now.

"Thanks for cooking for me," he finally said.

Rebecca flashed him a quick smile.

"You're welcome."

She dropped her arms and brushed by him towards the front exit.

That's my cue, he guessed and followed her. She opened the door for him. Tory took in her form, her beautiful face, her sexy body, wishing he could stay. But he understood the demands she had on her.

"I really do enjoy spending time with you. I hope you know that," he said, taking her hand in his.

Rebecca smiled sadly. She pulled her hand back and pecked his cheek.

"I know," she said, then added, "Good-night Tory."

Thirteen

ISOBEL SAT NERVOUSLY IN THE clinic waiting room. Being there made her feel as though her pregnancy was finally real. It was one thing to miss a period and assume pregnancy; it was something quite different to get confirmation and find out for certain that she was indeed carrying a new life. The mere thought caused her stomach to flutter, like a thousand tiny butterflies were flapping their wings.

Well, that and the fact that she was in the building next to the pediatric clinic where Tory worked. She had taken every precaution to make sure she didn't run into him, but still, there was always a chance she might. She didn't have a choice though, given the fact that she was there only because of charity.

"Isobel Mehilla," a nurse called, chart in hand. Isobel looked up. She had given them her mother's maiden name, in case any of them knew Tory. She stood up, collected her belongings and followed the nurse.

They walked back to an examination room, where the woman took her vitals and advised her doctor would with her shortly— all without any extraneous words, emotions or eye contact. The woman was obviously overworked. Isobel simply smiled and sat back on the examination table, not wanting to add to the nurse's stress. She picked up a magazine and tried to read the articles therein. When she couldn't muster enough interest in them, she flipped through the pages and looked at the pictures. Isobel stopped at the recipes and found one for a summer mango salad that sounded good.

I'll make it for Tory, she thought; and made a mental note of the ingredients.

Isobel looked through three more magazines before giving into the boredom of waiting. She reclined back, her body aching from sitting up straight for so long and stared out of the windows. She had a view of the parking lot, and beyond it, an empty field with overgrown shrubs and a sign advertising the acreage for sale. The clinic itself was new; construction had started before she left, so she knew the lot wouldn't be vacant for too much longer.

When she grew tired of gazing out the window, Isobel considered taking a nap. She had already been there an hour without a sign of the nurse or doctor. She wasn't going to complain though, she was there by mercy and nothing else; she wasn't the one footing the bill for the visit.

Still, she couldn't help but hope that Tory didn't keep his patients waiting like this. She knew the clientele for both clinics were lower and no income folks, but that didn't give the hospital staff a right to waste their time. Isobel was just lucky she had nowhere to be. Nancy had told her to come in the following morning. Apparently, she knew about the waiting time at the clinic.

"Well, how are we today?" a young doctor said, with a quick knock on the slightly opened door. He was no older than Tory and Isobel had to wonder if maybe they knew each other.

"Fine," she said as she sat up.

He sat down on the stool, reading over her chart and asking her questions she already answered: Yes, her period was overdue. No, she had not been to a doctor yet. No, she didn't drink anymore, No, she didn't smoke or ingest any illegal substances.

When the questions were done, he had her sit back and asked the nurse to bring in the ultrasound machine. Isobel said nothing and obeyed, watching as the same nurse came in, pushing the machine with her. The doctor disappeared down the hall for a moment before returning. Then the nurse instructed her to push her shirt up and her pants down so that her abdomen was visible. She tucked a towel into Isobel's pants and squeezed a cold lubricant onto her belly. The doctor meanwhile was talking to her about what she should expect, but she stopped listening when he placed the wand on her belly and moved it around. She heard what sounded like underwater pulses. The doctor applied more pressure to her abdomen and the sound became clearer. Steady. Strong.

"That's the heart," the doctor said, with a smile on his face.

Isobel looked up at him in disbelief. She listened to the beat, thumping like a drum, from deep within her. It was miraculous. A cliché, she knew, but true, nonetheless.

The doctor was talking to the nurse, who was taking down notes, when Isobel finally returned to reality. He replaced the wand on the cart and handed Isobel a towel to wipe off her wet belly.

"You're approximately fourteen weeks along. We'll get some blood work from you today and schedule you to come in once a month for now," he said as though reading from a script.

He probably does this so often, he's jaded, she thought.

"Congratulations," he said, with a hand on her shoulder. He gave her a brief smile and walked out. The nurse followed him, leaving Isobel to clean up. She didn't move for a moment, the steady beat of her baby's heart still echoing in her head. Hearing it gave her even more reason to get her life in order. Her baby deserved it.

After checking out, Isobel left the facility. She thought about going back to the apartment, but she was too excited. She needed someone to talk to, but not Pastor Martin and certainly not Tory. She was still shocked that he agreed to let her stay, but she couldn't get past the pain of knowing Tory had a girlfriend.

Ugh. The very words left a bitter taste in her mouth. Tory with a girlfriend. But she could hardly expect him to stay celibate and unattached for her. He had every right to live his life and move forward. So, what if they were still married. It was a technicality and time for her to take responsibility for all the pain she caused. She hadn't sought a divorce before, but maybe it was time to do so. Perhaps then Tory might forgive her.

No, she wasn't trying to buy his mercy, she wanted it uncontrived. The divorce was just something that needed to be done even if she didn't want it, even if he couldn't forgive her. Isobel was done stringing him along. She loved him enough to let him go.

Do you? came the accusatory voice.

Isobel didn't acknowledge it. Instead she looked at her watch, trying to determine if she had enough time to visit with Nancy. It was late in the afternoon, but the woman didn't keep set hours, and like Pastor Martin, would likely be found in her office, regardless of the time.

Thirty minutes later, Isobel arrived at the shelter. She was greeted at the door by the receptionist and was told Nancy was in her office. Isobel smiled to herself as she made her way back, liking the familiarity of her surroundings. Maybe there was something to the faithfulness Pastor Martin spoke of.

"So, how did it go, honey?" Nancy asked when she walked in. The older woman dropped everything she was doing and gave Isobel her complete attention.

With her hands on her belly, Isobel gushed, "I got to hear the baby's heartbeat. It was so amazing." She took a seat in the chair beside the desk as Nancy squealed with delight.

"Yes, it is. Oh, and they have such new technology today, far more advanced than when I was pregnant. When do you go back for a full ultrasound?"

"In a few weeks. I've got a routine check-up before then."

Nancy sat back and smiled at Isobel.

"Are you going to find out what the child's sex is?"

Isobel shrugged her shoulders.

"I'd like to. It'd be nice to know ahead of time."

"Any names you prefer?"

Isobel shook her head.

"Well, you've got a lot to think about then. I mean, more than you do already, right?"

"I guess so."

"Honey, do me a favor and just think about talking to Pastor Martin about this. He would want to know so he can pray for you, just as I do."

Nancy's tone didn't change from one subject matter to the other, catching Isobel by surprise. Truthfully, she had no aversion to telling the pastor, but for Tory. He couldn't know. It would only complicate matters.

But she couldn't deny Nancy her request either. The woman had become a friend and was only looking out for her.

"I'll think about it."

Nancy clapped her hands together.

"Thank you, dear. And actually, I'm glad you stopped by. I have a bit of good news for you." She turned back to her desk and started rummaging through her papers. "You're aware of our jobs program here. Well, I talked a former resident. She owns a bakery and restaurant; and needs someone to help her on the business side of things." Nancy found the sheet she was looking for and held it out to Isobel. "That's a description on what kind of help she needs: admin work, bookkeeping, that type of thing. Honestly, I think you're more than qualified, but the decision is up to you."

Isobel hesitantly accepted the paper, not because she didn't want the job, but because everything was happening so quickly. She didn't have to know what the job entailed— she was ready to say yes.

"I told her a little bit about you, I hope you don't mind. She's willing to work with you, if you want the job."

"She doesn't want to interview me first?" Isobel asked incredulously.

Nancy smiled.

"Well, certainly she wants to meet you, but she trusts me when I say I have met the most incredible young lady who is managing her situation with grace and strength and would make the perfect assistant."

Isobel frowned.

"But...I'm hardly...those things," she muttered.

"Oh, I don't know," Nancy countered, sliding her chair up to where Isobel was sitting.

"Oftentimes we create the demons that blind us from the truth. And the truth is that you are strong and faithful and dependable. I don't know who you used to be, but I know who you are now."

She took hold of Isobel's free hand and squeezed it. Isobel, though, didn't know what to say; neither could she stop the tears from rolling down the face. *Damn these hormones,* she thought as she quickly wiped them away.

Nancy let out a soft laugh.

"I do believe I've stunned you, haven't I?"

Isobel smiled sheepishly. Nancy rested her hand on her cheek. "It's quite alright. Sometimes it's good to let others tell you what they see."

ISOBEL ARRIVED back at Tory's apartment later that evening, feeling elated. She didn't know which she was more excited over, the job or the baby, but it didn't matter. Things were finally starting to look up. She would meet her new boss this week and start on Monday, meaning she could start looking for her own place soon. Tory would certainly be happy about that. She couldn't wait to share the news with him.

When she walked in though, Isobel knew something was wrong. All the lights were off, and Tory was on the phone in his bedroom.

His voice was muffled, but she could pick up a few words here and there.

Rebecca, please...it's not like that, you're overreacting...you're the only one I want...

A pang of guilt invaded Isobel's heart. Tory was having trouble with his girlfriend because of her. She hated the thought of Tory being with another woman, but she despised the idea that she was ruining Tory's life again even more. He had the perfect woman in every way, shape and form. Certainly, someone his mother would approve of. She made Tory happy. He definitely looked happy the day she saw them, and it was apparent the woman probably loved Tory the way he deserved to be loved.

All of a sudden, Isobel's head started hurting. Her stomach soured and she did all she could not to vomit. The temptation to leave was strong, but she had to be faithful. What was it Pastor Martin had said?

Be faithful to who you were created to be.

She was strong and faithful and dependable. That's what Nancy said.

If you were really all those things, you wouldn't have run in the first place. You wouldn't have a child who was conceived in lust and whose father is an abusive prick.

Laying a hand on her belly, Isobel recalled the heartbeat she'd heard earlier that day—the heartbeat of the child growing in her. A child who was still perfect and whose future was undetermined as of yet. The same could apply to her, couldn't it? She had hopes for herself, inasmuch as she did for her child. Her past didn't have to determine who she would be. She didn't have to run anymore. She didn't have to hide. She could be faithful. She could be.

Fourteen

"WHAT'S WRONG WITH you?" Charlie asked, as he lit up a cigarette. Tory was taking a break outside in the picnic area when his friend approached him. The grounds were smoke-free, but Charlie had no inhibitions about breaking the rules when there was no one around.

"You're gonna get caught one of these days," Tory muttered as he moved away from Charlie to avoid the smoke.

"They haven't caught me yet. And you didn't answer my question."

Tory shook his head.

"Nothing, alright?"

He could feel Charlie scrutinizing him.

"You're a bad liar, you know that?" Charlie said, blowing smoke out of his mouth and nose.

"Sorry, I'm out of practice. Remind me later to get with you on that and you can give me a refresher course."

"You're also an ass when you're in a bad mood."

"I didn't ask you out here," Tory retorted. He wasn't going to deny that he was moody; he just didn't want to be reminded of it.

"Yeah, well, I'm out here because I'm your friend. And I hate to see you like this. The psycho ex getting to you?"

Tory rolled his eyes.

"No."

And she wasn't. In the month she had been with him, Isobel managed to clean his apartment, stock the fridge and pack a few extra pounds on both of them. She did whatever she did during the day and made herself scarce at night. Sometimes he would talk to her about his day, other times he simply thanked her for cooking or for listening. It was a comfortable routine that even in its simplicity complicated every other aspect of his life. Especially the one where he was keen on pursuing Rebecca.

After their dinner date, she put distance between them, arguing that he was still stuck on his ex-wife. Why couldn't she see that he was only helping her for old time's sake—no, for Pastor Martin's sake? It bothered him immensely that she couldn't trust him. Why did she have to second-guess his decision, just as his parents did, just as Charlie was doing now? It seemed no one trusted him, except Isobel.

"Look, I'm not here to tell you what to do—" Charlie continued.

Tory cut him off.

"Yes, you are."

"Okay, I am, but we all know you're going to do whatever you want to do anyway—"

"So why are you really out here then?"

Charlie stubbed out his cigarette on the side of the bench and stuck the butt in his pocket. He sat down beside Tory.

"Is this your way of getting back at her? Or making up for the past few years? Because no one is worth that much trouble."

Tory stood up and, in a huff, exclaimed, "Why can't anyone just understand?"

He walked back to his office, ignoring the nurses as he wandered by them. He was still on his lunch break, so he shut the door and sat back in his chair. He had barely enough time to close his eyes when there was a knock on his door. Sure, it was Charlie, he stood up and snatched the door open.

"What?"

It was Rebecca.

"What are you doing here?" He could've kicked himself. "I'm sorry, come in."

She offered him a smile as she walked by him. Even dressed in her full uniform, her golden hair back in a bun, Rebecca was a sight to behold. He was appreciating her form when she turned back to him.

"I'm glad you stopped by," Tory said, closing the door. "You look great."

"Thanks," she replied. "I just wanted to follow up with you on that matter with your ex."

Tory frowned until she pulled out the business card he had given her. The favor he had asked of her. Apparently, the only reason she was there.

"I couldn't find anything on her. I found several reports of assault on a police officer in the past few months, but Isobel didn't fit the description of any of them." Rebecca flipped the card through her fingers, then handed it back to him. "Sorry I can't give you more."

Tory took the card from her, staring at it as though it might offer more information than Rebecca had given him. Not that he wanted to spend too much time thinking about it now, he'd do that later. Surely this was something he needed to share with Isobel. Now that he had Rebecca here with him though...

"Thank you," he said looking back to her.

"Anytime," she replied, and just as suddenly as she appeared in his office, she turned to disappear. Tory grabbed her arm before she could go.

"I want to see you, Rebecca."

She shook her head.

"I don't think that's a good idea."

"Why not?"

"Because Isobel is still a big part of your life."

Tory opened his mouth to argue, but she placed her free hand on his lips to silence him.

"Tory, listen. You are a nice guy, you really are. You're caring and giving and loyal. Any woman would count herself lucky to have your heart. But only one woman does. I don't know what the situation is between you and your ex, but I do know that Isobel left a hole in your heart that I will never be able to fill, and I would rather let you go now before I allow myself to believe I could mean that much to you."

He could hear the sorrow in her voice as she spoke and hated that she even had to think the words. He squeezed her hand and pulled her to him. But she resisted, pushing against his chest just hard enough to show him that she meant what she said.

"Rebecca, please," he pleaded.

"It's better this way," she said, her eyes shimmery. She blinked a couple of times and offered him a sad smile. "Goodbye, Tory."

Pulling her hand free, Rebecca turned away from him and walked out of his office,

leaving Tory standing alone and miserable—
no different than how she found him but
somehow worse than before. After the
realization of the moment hit him, Tory
found his way back to his chair and sat back,
closing his eyes again and wishing he was the
one that could run away.

IT WAS six in the morning when Isobel's
alarm went off. After washing up and
brushing her teeth, she went to the kitchen to
brew coffee. Since becoming pregnant the
smell of the black liquid was enough to make
her gag, but she was happy to fix it for others.
She found an insulated mug and with the
brew in hand, Isobel went outside to the front
step and sat down. The sun lighted on the
horizon, changing the dark sky to a purple
hue. The early morning air was crisp, and she
could see her breath, but she didn't mind. Her
internal temperature was all over the place
lately; when she should have been cold, she
was warm and vice versa. It was the
hormones for sure.

Still, it only helped her this morning as
she waited on Tory. He was on-call at the
hospital and due to get off soon. She knew he
would be wound up from being up all night.

That was his mode of operation before she left. Isobel couldn't imagine it had changed. If not, certainly the coffee and the company would help him unwind that much faster.

Maybe just the coffee. She wasn't sure he'd want the company.

Then again, with all the caffeine in the coffee, maybe she should have gone with tea. Tea was more calming. Did Tory even drink tea though?

"What you are you doing up?"

Isobel looked up at the sound of Tory's voice. She met his eyes for a moment, then looked down at the coffee cup in her hands. She should have gotten tea.

"I thought maybe you could use some com…ah…couh…coffee after working overnight," she said. "I remembered how it always took you a while to unwind."

Tory stopped in front of her and starred at her offering. He had not spoken to her in the week since she'd gone to the doctor; neither had she seen much of him. He either worked late or was not around.

After another quiet moment, Tory finally sat down beside her on the step, taking the mug. He held the cup with both hands, no doubt appreciative of its warmth.

"We can go inside…," she suggested, but he shook his head.

"This is fine," he said.

Isobel nodded. The sounds of morning drew her attention: car horns blaring, doors slamming, a fire truck in the distance, children talking—it was all distracting, which was fine with her, since she wasn't looking forward to the other reason for her being out there. Dread filled her while her heartbeat increased. She actually felt hot.

But she made it this far, she had to finish. Clearing her throat, Isobel spoke: "Tory, I'm sorry about...your girlfriend. If there's anything I can do to help mend things between you and...Rebecca, I'll do it."

There. She had done it: she had apologized to her husband about running off his girlfriend. Her life was officially ridiculous, but it was the least she could do.

Tory again shook his head though.

"No, it's not your fault," he muttered, turning the coffee cup in his hand. He had yet to drink from it. "We weren't dating, really..." Though his expression was blank, it was apparent he was hurting. He continued: "Listen, as long as we're on the subject, I owe you an apology for bringing her here that first week. That was insensitive on my part."

Tory moved his feet apart, widening his legs, and sat back against the door. He inadvertently nudged Isobel's knee. The simple touch made her heart race.

"Don't apologize," Isobel began, moving away from him. "This whole situation is..."

Her voice trailed off for lack of words. Tory seemed to understand what she couldn't say and nodded.

Silence fell between them. Lately Tory was the one starting or carrying the conversation; now that he wasn't, Isobel struggled to fill the quiet.

"I got a job," she managed.

He finally made eye contact, turning his head towards her.

"Yeah?"

She nodded.

"Nancy recommended me to Karen Ortiz, the owner of *Casa de la Panadería* downtown. I'm working as her assistant doing office stuff. It's part-time for now, but I've got room to grow as the business expands."

"That's great," he said, the sincerity in his voice unmistakable.

"And now that I'm employed, I'll be getting my own apartment soon. I'll be out of your hair before you know it."

"So, does that mean you're staying?"

Isobel hadn't really thought about it, but now as she considered his question, she realized perhaps she was planting herself. She knew she would eventually settle down because of the baby, but here, in the same town as Tory? Was that really what she wanted?

"I don't know," she replied, quietly.

Tory set the coffee cup down on the ground between them.

"Can I ask you something?" he asked.

Isobel's heart began pounding. She knew what was coming.

"Sure," she said anyway.

Again, he seemed to hesitate, fidgeting with his fingers, looking everywhere except her. Finally, he asked, "Why did you go?"

Isobel swallowed hard. She had been dreading this moment, having to explain herself. Oh, she was willing to admit her wrong, but no excuse seemed adequate enough for her actions.

"What did I do to push you away, Isobel? What happened to us?" he continued.

His voice was strained, and his words laced with an underlying anger—but not at her. Incredibly, he was mad at himself.

But telling him it wasn't his fault wasn't something he wanted to hear. After everything that happened with her and with Rebecca, he needed more. He needed something that could give him peace and assure him it wouldn't happen again. After all, nice guys finished last, didn't they? And Tory was the nicest guy she knew.

"Well," she began, and before she could stop the words from coming out of her mouth, she said, "It was your laundry habits." Isobel panicked for a moment; David never liked her sarcasm. Her comments were often met with a well-placed backhand. But Tory wasn't David. And when he smiled, Isobel relaxed.

"Laundry, huh?" he said.

"Yep. Remember that little black dress of mine you ruined? It was all downhill after that."

He laughed. Isobel couldn't help but laugh with him.

"In my defense, there was no label on that dress. It was black; it went in with the darks," he said. The laughter lifted the tiredness from his face. He was still so handsome. Isobel wanted to reach out and touch him, but she didn't dare.

Eventually the laughter died down though, leaving a silence the size of a city block between them. She sighed, thinking about the story Pastor Martin told her. Like the husband, Tory was long-suffering, undeserving of the torture she had put him through. He was entitled, if nothing else, to know why she left.

How could she adequately explain the biggest mistake of her life though? Because of her upbringing, Isobel always hoped for some kind of happy ending, but she didn't know how to achieve it. And she didn't know how to get beyond the things that seemed impossible, like settling down, being a wife, planning a budget, dealing with the idiosyncrasies of marriage. She loved Tory, but she couldn't see herself living the life of a domestic goddess. Isobel felt trapped. There were days she felt like she was suffocating and the longer she stayed, the worse it became. So, she made the decision to walk away and be free. It was anything but freedom though and she regretted her actions since leaving. She should have tried to change, tried to stay, but she chose the easy way out and was now dealing with the consequences of her actions.

"Tory, I…," Isobel started but no other words followed.

"Was there someone else?" he asked, still probing.

"No." Her answer was quick, honest, but it did nothing to assuage his heartache. She was having the opposite effect on him than what she hoped to instill, and she hated herself for it.

So much for helping him unwind.

Eventually, Tory stood up and stretched. Isobel watched as he bent back down to retrieve his coffee.

"Thanks for the coffee," he said softly, then added, "And for the company."

Then he went inside.

Fifteen

KAREN ORTIZ, A ROBUST LATINA with an infectious smile and pleasant voice, dropped the box on the desk with a loud thump.

"That's the last of them," Karen said, wiping her brow on her sleeve. "Obviously filing was not my specialty."

Isobel chuckled from behind the desk. In the past week of working with the woman, she learned that Karen preferred the lighter side of things, a joke or a funny story, but she was also very business minded. She knew what she wanted and pursued it with a passion; unfortunately, her admin skills were sorely lacking. The boxes contained files, receipts, and other important documents that Karen had kept since opening *Casa de la Panaderia*. Now it was Isobel's responsibility to file it all.

Karen plopped down on the chair in front of the desk. She was usually the first to arrive at the *panaderia* to turn on the ovens and start proofing the bread that would be used in making the different *pastelles* and *pan dulces;* as well as marinating the meats for the various meals that were served on the restaurant side of the business. It started off as a bakery, but slowly and surely grew as Karen added dishes from her childhood: *papa rellena, paella, sopa de tortilla* and *arroz con frijoles*. They were all simple meals, no different than the ones Isobel grew up on, but incredibly delicious. Though the place was no longer just a bakery, the name stuck. House of Bread, it translated into, and Isobel loved working there. Being an assistant was not her first choice, but because she was able to sample the foods, talk to the chefs and watch how the foods were prepared, it was the next best thing to the perfect job. Plus, it always smelled like bread. Nothing could beat that.

"Think you can handle all this?" Karen asked her.

Isobel smiled and nodded her head.

"It'll be a cake-walk," she insisted, keeping her tone light, confident. She wanted to impress Karen. The woman had taken a chance on her and Isobel didn't want to take that kind of trust for granted.

Karen chuckled.

"I like that. Cake-walk…Holler then if you need anything."

"I'll get it done," Isobel assured her.

"I know you will, *cariña*," she said, tiredness creeping into her voice. She had put in a long day already and still wasn't finished. With a stretch and a yawn, Karen exited, leaving Isobel to sort through years of unfiled paperwork. Paper by paper, sheet by sheet, she got to learn about the business and the woman who was now her boss. It wasn't until Karen came back a couple of hours later that Isobel realized how long she had been there.

"Find anything interesting?" Karen asked back in the same chair she vacated earlier.

Isobel shrugged her shoulders.

"It's alright. Standard stuff, you know? But the more you go through it, the more you understand about the people and business behind the business."

Karen smiled in amusement as Isobel cleared up the stack she was working on. It was time to go.

"So now you're a shrink?"

"No." Isobel blushed. "Hardly. Nothing like that. Just stuff I picked up in college. I took some classes, never finished though."

"Why didn't you finish?"

"I don't know. I wasn't a very good student, I guess."

"So, what did you end up doing?" Karen asked.

Isobel was usually reserved, so this line of questioning was uncomfortable. But she felt obliged to answer.

"Different things. Sales, retail, food, office temp. Whatever was available at the time."

"So, what do you really want to do?"

Isobel had a quick answer for everything but that. In the past, in her former life, she projected a confident exterior and attitude towards everything, but on the inside, she was unsure of herself and what she wanted from life. No, insecure was the better word. Now she was unconfident all around and while she would have loved to give Karen a different response, all she could say was, "I don't know."

Karen shook her head in disbelief.

"Well, we'll have to work on that, won't we?" she said as she rose to her feet. "But not today. You need to go home, and to be frank, so do I."

Isobel chuckled. With a "see you tomorrow," they parted ways. Isobel started towards the bus station, pondering what to fix for dinner when she noticed an older gentleman approaching her. Tall and slim, his hair greying at the roots. As he got closer, Isobel realized who he was. It was Henry, Tory's father and Sarah's husband. She stopped walking, her heart pounding faster and harder.

"Mr. Jamison," Isobel stated with apprehension. She wanted to run, bolt, hide, disappear, do all the things she promised herself she would never do again. Surely that was forgivable, considering the circumstances. After all, if Sarah was still upset with her, Henry couldn't be any happier.

But if he was, he had a funny way of showing it.

"Isobel," he said, as he stopped in front of her, his six-foot frame looming over her. With a big smile on his face, he exclaimed, "What a surprise!" Then he bent down and hugged her. Isobel was unsettled. But then, wasn't that Henry? He and Sarah were as different as night and day, especially where she was concerned. Henry had always been supportive of her, insisting she call him 'Dad' and Sarah 'Mom', while Sarah remained distant. He accepted her while Sarah gave her push-back. He was the one with the affection when Sarah denied her even a hug on her wedding day. He was...Henry. And he deserved a better response than paranoia and guilt.

Isobel let the man embrace her, happy at least one of the Jamison's didn't hate her.

"I don't think we need to be so formal, do you? I am still your father-in-law, aren't I?"

Her eyebrows shot up.

"Don't look so shocked, my dear. My son was always lazy when it came to doing what he didn't want to do, and Tory never wanted to admit his marriage failed." He took in her form, changing the subject. "So, let me see you. You've put on some weight..."

Isobel froze up. Could he tell she was pregnant?

"You look good. Healthy."

She relaxed for a moment and released the breath she had been holding.

"Are you hungry? I was about to grab something to eat."

It took her a moment to find her voice.

"No, thanks."

"Come on. Indulge an old man. I insist."

His tone wasn't threatening; even still, Isobel knew she couldn't argue.

"Alright."

They walked over to a small restaurant around the corner that served Lebanese food. Inside, the atmosphere was warm and inviting. The smell of warm pita bread filled her lungs, making her mouth water. After the waiter brought their drinks and an appetizer of bread and olive oil, Henry sat back in his chair, gazing at her.

"I have a confession to make," Henry said. "I didn't just run into you. Obviously, I knew you were back. I was waiting to see you."

"Why?" she asked, confused. Was she going to have to reconsider her opinion of Henry?

He hesitated for a moment. But only a moment. "I wanted to find out what your plans are, if you're staying."

The question of the hour. She had no answer for him though. Mainly because she had no answer period.

"So, are you back?" he asked again. "You are still family, you know. You're as much our daughter as Tory is our son."

Isobel couldn't help but scoff at his remark.

"Not to Sarah."

"Sarah was out of line in what she said and did, and I hope you will accept my apology for her. She had the best intentions at heart. Though that's hardly an excuse. But if you intend to stay, we deserve to know. Tory deserves to know. He loves you, you know."

Isobel shook her head.

"Maybe he did before, but not now, not after what I did to him. Something like that can't be fixed with 'I'm sorry'."

Henry gazed at her, almost sympathetically. He wasn't buying her argument.

"Tory doesn't love me," she insisted. "He's just being charitable."

"Why is he being charitable then?"

Isobel shrugged.

"Because you raised him right?"

Caught off guard, Henry gave her a hearty laugh.

"Yes, we did. But I can tell you there is more than just charity there. You're the only woman he's ever loved; the only one who ever made him truly happy. He may not show it right now, but that part of him has not changed in the four years you were gone. "

Isobel wasn't sure which was worse, Sarah yelling at her or Henry baiting her with love. Either way, it didn't matter what she wanted. Leave or stay in the area, the best she could hope for was Tory's forgiveness.

"Why don't you just think about it, Isobel? Don't give me an answer today. Let's just enjoy dinner and afterward, I'll give you a ride back to the apartment."

Sixteen

TORY WOKE UP BEFORE HIS alarm sounded. While this was normally annoying, today it was a good thing; he was in need of a shower and a shave after falling asleep in his work clothes. He preferred to come home and change, to keep the two areas of his life separate—work being work and his personal life being …whatever—sometimes though, there was overlap he couldn't avoid.

Or he could, if he cared.

He sat up, turned the alarm off, and peeled out of his shirt. He made his way to the bathroom, his limbs feeling twenty pounds heavier. He stretched and peered at himself in the mirror. There were bags under his eyes, and he looked ten years older. And that beard…Tory scratched his chin, looking at the growth. He had always been clean-shaven, like his father. He never even really thought about growing a beard. But one lazy day turned into two, and one week later, his face was covered. It didn't look bad though. He had thought to shave it, out of habit of course, but now that he looked at it, Tory decided to leave it.

He took his time showering and getting dressed. Tory could hear Isobel in the kitchen, washing dishes and fixing breakfast. The aroma of cooked bacon and fresh coffee wafted through the apartment, making his stomach growl with hunger.

In the kitchen, Tory sat in his usual spot at the counter to eat, while Isobel finished cleaning. He could tell she was running late by the way she rushed. As of lately, there very few words exchanged between them, but then, it wasn't like they needed to speak. They were like two old married people, living routine lives.

Tory watched Isobel. She didn't avoid eye contact like she did when she first arrived, but she was still reserved around him. Except for that morning when she waited for him to come home after he worked overnight, she kept to herself. Which was good, he supposed, considering how unceremoniously cranky he'd been lately. He kept hoping, like last time, that Rebecca was simply upset and would eventually call once she'd calmed down, but it never happened. Things were over between them.

Not that there was much to be over with, since they'd never really dated. If he was completely honest, he'd admit his ego took a bigger hit than his heart did. Maybe he just wanted love for love's sake.

The biggest surprise in all this though was Isobel's willingness to speak to Rebecca. That was, well, crazy, but it also spoke volumes about how much she had changed. The old Isobel would never have done that for anyone, much less him. Never.

Isobel wiped her hands on a towel and looked around to make sure everything was the way it should be. Then she went to her room to get her things. Her shirt was snug: she had put on a little more weight, especially in her breasts. They were full and heavy. He wondered how they would feel in his hands.

Shaking the thought off, Tory turned back to his food.

How could you even think of Isobel like that? Remember, she's the one who left. And she can't even tell you why.

Tory ignored that particular argument. It had lost its strength and no longer held the same power as when Isobel first arrived. Perhaps he had finally forgiven her.

How about this one then? What's she been doing for the past four years? Are you really going to help her so she can run into the arms of another man?

Now this precise question, he had no answer for. Though he had questioned her the other morning about why she left, part of him just didn't care where she'd been. He didn't want to know. But that's when doubt crept in: what was going to happen between them? Was there anything happening between then? Was she back? Or just here because it was familiar? Maybe she had moved past him? Maybe he had moved past her? Maybe they were reconnecting? Maybe he still loved her...

No.

So why did the thought of her with another man make him sick? Perhaps something did remain, and he was simply in denial. They were still married, after all. Though he had threatened to file for a divorce, Tory never did; and he really hadn't given much thought to it since then. He was just lazy like that.

Or you just don't want to let Isobel go...

No.

Maybe then Isobel doesn't want to let you go...

Based on her silence on the matter, Tory could only speculate she hadn't made plans to divorce him either, but she was working on finding an apartment and moving out. Maybe it was just what remained of his love that had him feeling empty already, but Tory had to concede: it's what was best. Regardless of the doubt and confusion, their marriage ended four years earlier when she left and all that remained was to make it official.

And if that was the case, then there was no point in asking her where she had been.

With a sigh, Tory turned back to the coffee Isobel made for him, just the way he liked it.

Isobel rushed into the living room, one shoe in hand, the other on her foot. She sat down on the couch long enough to put it on before grabbing her purse.

"Do you want a ride?" Tory asked her. He wasn't sure why he offered. His mouth seemed to be operating on its own volition without thought to what *he* wanted to do.

Isobel stopped and gazed at him.

"I'm done. We could leave now," he added.

"You're driving in?"

He hadn't planned on it, but now that she mentioned it, he couldn't very well place her on the handlebars of his bike, could he? A beautiful hood ornament no doubt, but not very practical.

"Yeah, thought I'd give the bike a break today."

She frowned.

"It's out of your way, are you sure?"

"Yeah," he replied, standing up and drinking the last of his coffee. "Come on."

Reluctantly she agreed and in minutes they were on their way. It was a short drive to the *panaderia* from the complex, but traffic made it longer...much longer. Tory could only imagine how long the trip took by bus.

As they inched along in traffic, Tory's mind kept going back to the questions he had been pondering earlier. Though he was preoccupied, he did notice Isobel glance at him every so often.

"What?" he finally asked.

She turned red and looked forward to the cars in front of them. He thought she might clam up, but she didn't.

"You look different with a beard. You look good."

Tory smiled at the compliment.

"Thanks."

There were a few more minutes of quiet between them before either spoke.

"I saw your father the other day," Isobel said.

Tory cringed, unsure if this was a good thing or not. He couldn't imagine his dad doing anything that would require an apology, but considering the current circumstances with Isobel's return, anything was possible.

"Do I need to apologize for him too?"

Isobel chuckled.

"No. It was fine. He was his usual self. Very direct, but sweet."

Tory nodded, and they fell quiet again. He didn't feel the need to fill the stillness with words when the ambience was…comfortable.

They didn't speak again until Tory pulled into the parking lot of the bakery and stopped near the door. Isobel grabbed her bag; and as she exited the car, she thanked him.

Tory nodded and waited until she was inside before he left. He didn't feel as tired or as heavy as he had that morning. Maybe he'd just slept too long.

MELISSA WAS holding up Hannah's chart when Tory walked into the clinic. He learned to recognize it from a distance, based on the thickness of it.

"What's wrong with Miss Hannah this morning?" he asked.

"It's her skin. Poor baby's not doing too well," the nurse said.

Tory dropped his things in his office, grabbed his stethoscope, and walked over to the examination room that Ashley and Hannah currently occupied.

Hannah squealed when she saw him and held out her toy, a pink car, for him to see. Tory, however, did not feel quite as enthusiastic as she did. There were long socks on her arms and legs, making her skin inaccessible to her nails. Her face was rosy, splotched red in the areas she had been scratching.

"Sorry to be in here so early," Ashley said. "Her skin's gotten worse and that cream you gave us last time just wasn't helping."

Tory shook his head as he washed his hands.

"Don't apologize. That's what I'm here for."

After drying up, he walked over to Hannah.

"Hey, beautiful," he cooed. "Mind if I take a look at your skin?"

She was distracted with her toy though and didn't respond. Tory took advantage of this and pulled one sock down off her knee. Her skin was red, raw, and broken. He winced as he looked at it, knowing how irritating it had to be that she scratched until she bled. He checked both legs and then her arms before replacing the socks and pulling the wheeled stool in front of her. Tory listened to Hannah's heart and lungs. She giggled when the stethoscope touched her skin and dropped her toy on the table. He retrieved it for her, and she seemed only then to realize he looked different. She held out her socked hand to touch his face and withdrew it quickly when she felt the prickly beard, giggling as she did.

Tory shook his head, laughing along with her.

"What are we going to do with you?" he posed, rhetorically.

Having satisfied her curiosity, Hannah returned to her toy. Careful to keep one hand on the table to corral her if necessary, Tory turned to Ashley. He could see the worry etched into her face. Being a single mom had to be hard enough; having to deal with this surely made the situation seem impossible at times. He marveled at her strength.

"I've got another cream I want you to try it, but again, it's a steroid, so use is limited."

Ashley's face dropped. Tory felt her disappointment. Even with all his knowledge and all the medicine accessible to him, he was limited in what he could do for Hannah—but he wasn't ready to give up on either of them. He knew after practicing medicine for years now that pharmaceutical drugs weren't the only answer.

"I know this is discouraging but hang in there. We'll figure this out. We'll change her diet, look at natural remedies. Whatever it takes. I'll do some research and have Melissa give you a call. Okay?"

Ashley sighed and nodded.

"Thank you, Dr. Jamison. I know it doesn't mean much, but I really am grateful."

"It's not meaningless. In fact, I thrive on hearing it over and over," he said, tongue-in-cheek, soliciting a laugh from her. "Hey, if Hannah can go through this with a laugh, we can too."

Ashley gave him an appreciative smile, then asked, "Do you have kids, Dr. Jamison?"

"No," he said, shaking his head. It was a dream long forgotten.

"I thought maybe you had a whole brood at home based on the way you handle Hannah."

Tory chuckled.

"No. I think Hannah just makes it easy."

Ashley laughed incredulously. Hannah joined in, laughing a high-pitched laugh that was contagious.

"Yeah, sure she does. Would that be before or after she's eaten baby wipes and rubber bands? Neither of which are digestible, by the way."

Again, Hannah laughed, not realizing she was laughing at herself. Tory couldn't help but join in.

When quiet finally settled over them, Ashley sighed and wistfully remarked, "You're right, of course. When she is not getting in trouble, Hannah is an angel. And I guess I wouldn't have it any other way. She is an amazing little person who makes me want to be the best mom I can be."

The mention of parenthood made Tory to think about Isobel. She had been reticent to have children when they first married, and he couldn't blame her: she didn't know what it was like to have a father and her mom was a sorry excuse for a human being. No one would want to be a parent with that kind of upbringing. But it was an argument she was never willing to revisit. Even though his dad treated her like a daughter and Tory assured her she would not be like her mother, Isobel still refused to consider the possibility of children. She shut the door on his dream and then left.

But she came back…

Uncomfortable with where his thoughts were headed, Tory excused himself to get Hannah's prescription sheet. He attempted to focus on anything but the nagging question in the back of his mind, demanding to know if his dream of being a father was still possible.

Seventeen

TORY TOOK ANOTHER SIP OF HIS coffee as he watched the morning news. It was the usual stuff—death, murder, mayhem—and the reason he had quit watching it. He had worked in the ER for several years and witnessed the worst of humanity on some nights. Watching the news only served as a reminder of that time. Unfortunately, he had to sit through it to get the traffic report. Tory has decided to hang up his bike for a while and drive to work. He still enjoyed biking, but he would find other times to cycle.

Isobel entered the living room, dressed for work.

"You ready?" he asked.

She met his gaze and nodded.

He had offered her a ride again today, and until further notice since he was no longer cycling to work, a decision he had made earlier that morning, when he dragged himself out of bed, tired. It seemed pointless to have her riding the bus when they could go together.

Tory rinsed out his coffee cup in the sink before depositing it in the dishwasher. Then he grabbed his keys and bag and led the way to his car. The commute was a quiet one until he dropped her off at the *panaderia.*

"Thank you," she said with a grateful smile and went inside.

Half an hour later, Tory was pulling into the parking lot of the clinic, feeling content. Traffic aside, it was shaping out to be a good morning and he was simply enjoying it for what it was.

"Well, someone's in a good mood," Melissa greeted him.

He shook his head.

"No more than usual."

The day went by fairly quickly. Between patients, Tory continued his research for Ashley and had Melissa call her as promised. He was still in a good mood when Charlie cornered him in the cafeteria during lunch and asked rather bluntly, "Are you screwing her?"

Tory wanted to be annoyed, he really did, but he was tired of it—tired of being upset, tired of explaining himself. So, he humored his friend instead.

"And by *her* you mean…?"

"Don't get coy with me, mister," Charlie remarked, dropping into the seat across from him. "You've been happy all day, like a kid in a candy store. You're screwing Isobel, aren't you? You're all in her goodies, aren't you?"

Tory gave the argument no thought. It seemed incredible to him that he could forgive Isobel and others couldn't. He was, after all, the one most wronged by her. What did it matter to them?

He popped the last morsel of food in his mouth and rose to his feet. No doubt giving Charlie plenty to think about, he picked up his tray and remarked before walking off, "You, my friend, are crass. I'll see you back in the clinic."

And he did, but there were no more words exchanged between them, just knowing glances. Allowing it no more thought than necessary, Tory finished up his duties, glad when the end of the day had arrived. He sat in traffic much too long and arrived home in time to find Isobel cooking dinner. The aroma that greeted him was amazing.

"What are you making?" he asked.

Isobel smiled.

"Sausage stuffed eggplant and creamy spinach pasta. It was one of *Abuelo's* recipes."

Her grandfather was the only family member Isobel ever spoke fondly of. He was unable to take custody of her after her mother left because of his declining health, but he was there for her as often as he could be. Once he died though, there was nothing Isobel had to stick around for. It had broken Tory's heart to hear what she had experienced as a child, but the stories she told about her grandfather made him wish he had met him.

"Everything's almost done," she said, grabbing a couple of plates.

Tory noted how she was still wearing her work clothes. He dropped his things and reached for the plates.

"I'll get that—you go get changed."

She gave him a cautious glance but obeyed. Doing what he had seen his wife do countless times, Tory plated the food, prepared two glasses of wine and set everything on the coffee table. He was going to have to invest in a dining table one of these days. He hadn't had much use for one before today, but it was probably a good thing to have now.

Tory grabbed some silverware and took the liberty of tasting the pasta. It melted in his mouth. Anxious to sit down and enjoy the meal, he ran to his room and quickly changed, throwing on a t-shirt and a pair of sweatpants – elastic sweatpants. He planned on having seconds.

Back in the kitchen, Tory grabbed some napkins and sat down on the couch to wait for Isobel. He turned the television on and found a movie to watch. Isobel came out a minute later looking refreshed. She almost had a glow about her.

"Sit down and eat," he said, as he picked up his fork and dug into the eggplant. Isobel joined him on the couch. "I don't know how you do it. I could take the same ingredients and never come close to this."

Isobel chuckled.

"*Abuelo* used to say that everyone could cook, but only some were gifted to create. You just have to know which one you are."

"So why are you doing admin work when your gift clearly lies in the kitchen?" Tory asked, taking another forkful.

Isobel was taken aback by the question, no doubt wondering where it came from. He wasn't sure. Part of him was ashamed to think he had never appreciated her food (or anything else she did for him) like this. But the other part of him didn't want to see her waste her potential now that she was trying.

"I don't know. I guess I was just trying to be grateful for the opportunity," she replied.

"That's great, don't get me wrong," he continued. "I'm just saying with talent like this"—he held up a forkful of eggplant— "it's a shame to let it go to waste."

She smiled.

"So, I'm wasting it on you?"

"Absolutely not!" he exclaimed with a laugh. Then allowed himself to get serious for a moment. "I'm just saying obviously this is the one good thing you got from your family. I don't know how you feel about it now…you know, as opposed to before you left…but maybe your grandfather left it to you so that you wouldn't be left without a way in this world."

Talking about her family was always a touchy subject if she didn't initiate it, but when Isobel offered him a small, appreciative smile, he knew she'd heard him.

The atmosphere settled into something warm, something familiar. The conversation continued as Isobel asked about Hannah and Tory inquired about her job. He replenished his plate and wine glass, offering to do the same for Isobel. She declined, saying she would let the food settle first, though she hadn't touched her wine.

Isobel pulled her feet onto the couch and tucked them underneath her, making herself comfortable as Tory ate. Both focused on the television. Tory finally reached his fill and put his fork down. He let out a heavy breath and sat back, feeling uncomfortable around his midsection. Isobel shook her head in amusement and let out a laugh. Tory made a face at her, nudging her leg with his hand and letting it rest on her knee. Yes, he'd made a glutton of himself. But some things were worth it and letting Isobel spoil him like this was definitely worth the extra five pounds he had likely gained.

The warmth of Isobel's skin beneath his hand brought back memories of how things used to be between them. The evenings together. The shared laughter. The intimate touches. And while they were good memories, they were also a reminder of the heart-aching reality of the moment. An overwhelming emptiness filled his soul and Tory was never more aware that something was missing than he was right now. That realization caused him to disconnect from Isobel. He placed his hand on the couch and turned back to the television, hoping, praying, he didn't appear as lonely as he felt.

IN THE past, there was only one way a night like this ended and that was with sex.

Except of course for that first night. Their first date.

Isobel had cooked for Tory, wanting to spoil him the way Latin women were apt to do of their men. Sure, he was out of her league, but he seemed genuinely interested in her. They spent the evening eating and talking and enjoying each other's company. He told her about his plans to become a pediatrician, while she listened. She was taken with his handsome features and his gentle nature. And when she talked, he stole her heart by listening. She had never been one to give up much on the first date, but she was ready to give it all to Tory if he asked.

He didn't though. The evening wrapped up, he kissed her on the cheek, and thanked her before going home, leaving her feeling empty inside.

Just like now.

She thought about Tory's hand on her knee. Sure, she knew what intimacy was, but there was just something about his touch that got her heart racing. Even when it was careless and accidental.

Oh, to feel something deliberate: the warmth of his skin heating hers, his heart beating with hers, his breath mingling with hers as they kissed, his hands roaming all over her body…her pregnant body.

And with that thought, Isobel was jerked back to reality.

You missed your chance, she reminded herself. *You gave Tory up.*

Saddened, Isobel rested her head on the back of the couch, her eyes on the television.

She had lost interest in the movie long ago and had no idea what was happening. She yawned. Her body was changing for the baby and while the process was awe-inspiring, it was also draining her of energy.

"Tired?"

Tory's voice was soft.

"A little," she said truthfully.

"Why don't you go to bed?"

Isobel shook her head.

"I gotta clean up.

"I'll do it," Tory said.

Isobel eyed him carefully, her heart heavy with the emotion of the evening. Tired of questioning his motives, Isobel gazed down at her hands and nodded her head.

"Alright," she said, her voice strained.

She pulled her feet out from under her and stood up. Tory was right behind her. She grabbed her plate and wine glass and started towards the kitchen.

"Leave it. I'll get it," Tory reiterated as he reached for her plate.

She turned around and let him take it. She was getting ready to say, 'thank you,' to appreciate his thoughtfulness and kind words, but she found herself lost in his eyes— his beautiful green eyes, eyes that captured her attention so many years before. And if she was honest, still did.

Then he leaned over and kissed her cheek.

"Thanks for spoiling me, Issie," Tory said.

A sob lodged itself in her throat, rendering her silent. She offered him a brief smile and quickly left to her room.

Eighteen

"GOOD NIGHT, DR. JAMISON," Melissa said as she walked by his office. She stopped long enough to wave at him before she left.

Tory gazed up for a moment, missing her completely, but yelling the obligatory response anyway.

"Have a good night."

His words trailed off as he returned to the paperwork in front of him. He stared at it for a moment longer before determining he had glared at it long enough. He wasn't accomplishing anything; and truth be told, he wasn't going to complete anything no matter how long he sat there.

Ever since he'd had dinner with Isobel a few days ago, he'd stayed later and later at work. No different than when she first arrived, but different in every way. He was being cautious: he couldn't be alone with her. In the morning in the car stuck in traffic was one thing. In the evening, in the apartment with her was quite another. Especially after that kiss. The one on her cheek. The one that still lingered on his lips. The one that was not content with just her face but wanted him to take her in his arms and remember all the things they used to do on evenings like that. Evenings that usually ended up in the bedroom with Tory loving every inch of her body. Oh, and there was more of it to love now. He would have never thought it possible, but she was more beautiful now than when they first met. The very thought filled him with desire, which was why he was so apprehensive to be with Isobel alone. Lust, love or denial—whatever it was—Tory wanted her.

But he couldn't be with her. He wasn't part of her future. Forget the other arguments about her leaving and betraying him. The fact remained: she was moving out when she found her own place and leaving him behind once again.

With a sigh, Tory collected his things and left. He wasn't going to get any work done thinking about Isobel. He proceeded to the main building, which was connected to the parking deck where his car was located. As he navigated the halls to the elevator that led him to the deck, Tory noticed a tall, commanding figure walking away from him towards the main exit. Tory stopped as an uncomfortable feeling settled over him. It was Detective Harris.

What's he doing here?

Tory heard his name called behind him. He turned around to see Dr. Hall, head of the pediatric department and Tory's mentor, standing in the doorway of his office. Tory looked back once more to the direction Harris was traveling but he was gone.

"Dr. Hall," Tory said as he approached the older man.

"Hey Tory. Come on in my office."

Tory followed him in, taking a seat when the man did.

"I take it you know the detective," Dr. Hall said.

"I've spoken to him once before."

"He was asking about you and your ex. Seems she's in trouble?"

Tory knew the older man and trusted him, but he didn't know what to make of this situation with Isobel and Detective Harris, much less how to explain it. Plus, he still had a hard time believing that Isobel had assaulted anyone.

"That's what he said."

"Tory, listen, you know I'm here to talk if you need to…"

Dr. Hall knew the sordid tale his marriage was. He had helped Tory through the initial period after Isobel left, when his job performance started suffering. He was grateful for his concern, but Tory needed to sort through this first before he spoke to anyone.

"I appreciate it, but I honestly don't know what this is about."

Dr. Hall appeared doubtful, but remarked, "Alright. You know my door is always open. How're things over at the clinic?"

"Busy," Tory replied, rising to his feet, not wanting to chit-chat. "But that never changes, right?"

"Wouldn't be a bad thing if it did," the man said, following his lead. "But then, kids and germs go together, don't they?"

Tory chuckled, thinking about Hannah. There were no recent visits, only a call to let him know Hannah's skin had improved with his recommendations. He was sure though he'd be seeing her soon.

"I told Detective Harris to go through official channels instead of wandering the halls," Doctor Hall added as they walked to the door. "Hopefully it'll be the end of that. But just call me if you need to."

The doctor bid him goodnight. Tory resumed his walk to the parking deck, his steps slower, heavier, than they were before. It was still light out, but night would be upon them soon, bringing with it the blanket of insecurity it usually did. Oh, everything seemed okay. He would go home as he normally did, and Isobel would have a fine meal waiting for him and they would play house for a while, but it wasn't all okay.

Tory pulled his keys out of his pocket and unlocked his car. He tossed his bag in and sat behind the wheel, lost in thought. Why was this whole ordeal so troubling? And why didn't he just ask Isobel about it?

Because you don't want to deal with the last four years.

He reached into his wallet and pulled out Detective Harris' business card. Tory stared at it, flipping it front and back, as if the card itself could spill all of the man's secrets. His dirty laundry. His obsession with Isobel. The motive behind the man's actions. The reason the man would travel as far as he had to find her…

Tory sighed. He may have been unwilling to address Isobel's past, but he could no longer deny it: Detective Harris had been involved with Isobel.

Tory sunk into the chair, his hands on his face. It was easier to forgive and accept Isobel when her absence lacked a face. Not so much now that he could see whom he had been replaced with.

David Harris. The man was daunting, and he had a certain presence about him. He seemed to be everything Tory was not. Was he what Isobel was searching for? Was he the real reason she left? Perhaps he could satisfy her in ways Tory could not.

Tory suddenly felt sick. How could he ever imagine that he was enough for a woman like Isobel? He had thought once that he was the luckiest man on the planet to call Isobel his own, but he was nothing but a distraction. A fool. Like his mother had said, Isobel had left him for the next guy with a bigger dick and bigger paycheck.

And Harris most likely had both.

Tory shut his eyes tight. He didn't want to think about Isobel anymore. He didn't want to picture her with the detective; he didn't want to wonder what it was the man did to draw her away from Tory. He just wanted to forget that Isobel ever came back, forget that she ever left.

That's right, she left you.

Not now.

Oh yeah, we're doing this now. She left you; then she left him.

Tory opened his eyes.

Think about it. Why else would he be looking for her? She left him.

So, what did that mean? Had she changed? Did she have a reason to leave? Or was she just doing what she'd always done?

He knew she wasn't playing games anymore; the old Isobel would have never humbled herself as she had done on more than one occasion. The old Isobel would have kept going. So why would she leave Harris then? Had she grown tired of him? Bigger dick and bigger paycheck didn't equal happiness?

Then Tory recalled the bruises he saw on her legs and back hours after her arrival. Anger boiled in him. Was that the reason she left? Had the man, big and intimidating as he was, struck Isobel?

Tory sat up and gripped the steering wheel, angry not so much with Harris, but with Isobel. Was this the man she traded him for? An ox who didn't know the difference between a woman and a punching bag? Tory had blamed himself for the longest time—if only he had done *this*, if only he had done *that*. The list was long. But he would have never hit Isobel. He would have never hurt her, never laid a finger on her except to love her. He would have protected her and loved her each and every day. He would have treated her the way she was meant to be treated.

So, what's stopping you from doing that now?

They lost four years; but why couldn't he do that for her now? Why couldn't he show her that he was better than any of the choices she made? He had promised her his love, his heart, and his life; always hoping she would one day come back to him. And now she had. Couldn't they work things out?

What if she wants the boyfriend back?

She left him.

But what if you're wrong? What if the bruises were from something else? What if her departure was just a misunderstanding? What if she finds out he's looking for her and he convinces her to go back with him? Can you stand to lose her again?

He didn't think he could. But if he did nothing then he had already lost her for good.

TORY PULLED his key out of the lock as he pushed open the door to his apartment. It was late. Really late. He'd meant to be home sooner but lost track of time.

That's what you get for arguing with yourself, he chastised himself.

Shutting the door quietly so as not to wake Isobel up, he stepped into the kitchen where the stove light cast a soft glow on everything within range. There was a covered dish on the counter. Isobel had set aside a plate for him. Tory couldn't see what was on it but going by the scent still lingering in the room, it was something meaty and spicy. Tory's heart warmed at the gesture; and though he had eaten already, his mouth watered.

Tory placed his bag on the counter, his keys beside it and was ready to take a peek at the plate when he noticed Isobel asleep on the couch. She was a wearing an oversized t-shirt and a pair of sweatpants. Her head was resting on a cushion and she was curled up tightly, her arms tucked in between her knees. She looked peaceful, beautiful.

Grabbing a throw blanket off of the loveseat, Tory covered her up. Isobel stirred slightly, causing him to stop, lest he wake her. She pulled the blanket closer to her. Tory knelt down in front of her and watched her sleep. Most of her hair had been pulled back in a ponytail, but there were a few stragglers hanging over her face. Gently, he tucked the silky strands behind her ear. He liked the look and feel of her hair now. Short was cute, but the longer style really complimented her.

Tory let the back of his hand graze her cheek. Her skin was so soft, so delicate, and so kissable. Yet he didn't dare.

Why not though? Hadn't he kissed her the other night? Hadn't he given himself permission to love her again just hours earlier? What was stopping him?

What if she doesn't love you?

Despite the positive change in their relationship, Isobel still remained distant, unsure and shy. Was she just there receiving his help so she could move on with her life? Or was it possible that she was still attracted to him? She did comment on his looks, his beard. And every once in a while, he would catch her staring at him. He stared at her that way, admiring her beautiful body, so maybe there was still an attraction there. Or maybe he was making something out of nothing. Maybe she was still attracted to the boyfriend. Maybe she wasn't ready for any kind of relationship at all.

Isobel sighed and moved against him. He withdrew his hand from her as her eyes gradually peeled open.

"Hey," he said softly. "I didn't mean to wake you."

She appeared confused for a moment, glaring at him with a frown on her face.

"What time is it?" she asked.

"About 1:30?" Tory guessed. It had been close to that time when he pulled into the apartment complex. "What are you doing out here?"

She sat up and back, away from him.

"I…," she began, and hesitated, as if she'd been caught doing something she shouldn't have.

Tory watched her, unsure of what to make of her behavior. She was genuine in her actions, but she seemed reticent around him, scared almost, like a timid little rabbit. Was this because of her relationship with Harris? Or something else altogether? She had never been like that before. Tory suddenly felt an overwhelming desire to scoop her up into his arms and keep her safe.

"I was…I guess I just fell asleep," Isobel murmured. She stretched and pulled the blanket closer to her when it dropped onto her lap. "I left you a plate on the counter. You've probably already eaten, but you can take it for lunch tomorrow…if you want."

"I'm off tomorrow," he remarked. Then an idea struck him. "Are you working tomorrow?"

She shook her head.

"Do you want to do something?" he asked, "Since we're both off, I mean? We could go out or something…if you want to, of course," he added.

Again, she was reluctant. Would she say no if she could read his mind? What he was really thinking? About her?

"Okay," Isobel finally said.

"Great." He took her hands in his and rose to his feet, taking her with him. The light from the kitchen illuminated her big eyes, her round face, her shapely figure. She was positively attractive.

Isobel pulled her hands from his.

"Good night, Tory."

She stepped back and picked up the blanket that had pooled around their ankles. Isobel turned towards her bedroom, but Tory called her back. With Isobel waiting on him, he asked, "Have you...found any place yet you might want to move to?"

It was a simple enough question, but if she said no, then perhaps with no prospects, she would consider staying with him.

He didn't even want to consider the situation if she said yes.

Isobel's figure stiffened. Skepticism, incredulity, and even suspicion, were all reflected on her face.

"No, not yet, but I'm working on it. I should have something really soon."

He noted how quickly she answered, the anxiety that suddenly filled her voice. He almost sighed with relief but didn't. All he needed to know was that she wasn't going anywhere anytime soon.

"I was just asking," he assured her. "I told you, you can stay as long as you need to."

Another moment passed between them before she quietly replied, "Thank you." Then she slipped away and went to bed.

Nineteen

ISOBEL OPENED HER EYES. SUNLIGHT was streaming in through the window. It was later than when she usually woke, but she'd been so tired lately, she needed the sleep. And she was glad. She felt refreshed. New.

The scent of bacon drifted through the air and her stomach growled. Isobel was ready to eat—or rather Isobel *and baby* were ready to eat. Her appetite had increased exponentially in the last week or so, making her wonder if the baby was not going through its first growth spurt. Isobel wasn't showing yet, except for the slight bump on her lower abdomen, but it wouldn't be long now.

Her stomach growled again.

Who was cooking? Tory? Isobel sat up. She'd always cooked for him, so what was he doing? Was he cooking because she slept late? He had said last night...

Oh, last night. Isobel suddenly remembered the events from the previous night. Tory coming home late, asking her if she had found an apartment yet. Was he trying to tell her it was time to go? Was he trying to gauge how soon it would be before he got his place back? Maybe he had met someone, someone who would do for him what she was doing now.

Isobel grimaced at her last thought. She had to constantly remind herself that it wasn't her responsibility any more to care for him and make sure he was taken care of. Regardless of what was written on their marriage license, they were not husband and wife and she could not afford to get attached to him, or rather, get any more attached. She loved Tory but if she got any closer to him than they were now, she would be leaving with a broken heart.

The irony.

Enough self-pity, she thought, it was time to get up and eat. She grabbed her toiletry items and headed to the bathroom. She stopped at the doorway long enough to hear Tory utter a curse when he dropped a pan on the floor. She couldn't help but giggle.

After washing up, Isobel wandered into the kitchen. Tory was standing at the counter muttering to himself, a sheepish expression on his face.

"This was supposed to be breakfast," he said apologetically. "Obviously I'm not the cook you are."

Isobel stifled a laugh when she saw the stack of burnt pancakes on the plate. He had crisped the outside of the fluffy pastry into a hard, black shell. An audible 'pop' drew their attention to the stove. Both turned around to see smoke starting to billow out from the skillet Tory was cooking bacon in. Before Isobel could warn him not to, he grabbed the handle of the frying pan and moved it to a back burner, burning his hand in the process. The reaction was delayed, but soon Tory let out a yell as his hand began turning red.

Isobel rushed over to Tory and pushed him over to the sink, where she ran the cold water. When the temperature was at its coldest, she placed Tory's hand beneath the frigid water. Then she ran to the bathroom and grabbed the tube of toothpaste. Tory was scowling when she returned to the kitchen. She turned the faucet off, gently took his hand in hers, and dried the excess water off. Then she picked up the toothpaste.

"Oh, not that," he moaned.

Isobel chuckled. Her grandfather had immigrated to the country when he was a young man in his twenties and subscribed to an *alternative* way of doing things: toothpaste for burns, ground coffee for cuts, onions for fevers, and many other home remedies. Tory didn't put much stock in any of it—he had always refused to partake of it—but they worked.

"Oh, hush and take your medicine like a big boy," she ribbed, leading him over to the stool, where she applied the toothpaste. He glowered at her, no doubt his pride wounded for having to allow her to treat him with oral hygiene paste, of all things.

What was the saying? Doctors make the worst patients? Boy, were they right.

Turning back to the stove, Isobel cut the burner off, covered the skillet and turned on the exhaust fan.

"So that was your plan for our day off? A trip to the emergency room?"

Tory sneered at her as she surveyed the greasy mess in front of her.

"You're the one who said anyone could cook."

"Nope, *Abuelo* said that. I never agreed with him."

"Ha, ha," he muttered dryly.

Isobel didn't hide her laughter as she ran the hot water and reached for the dish soap. Everything was covered in a layer of bacon fat. And none of the food was edible.

"How did you survive without me?" Isobel commented and instantly regretted the words as they escaped her mouth. They were meant in jest. Mindlessly spoken in a moment of levity. But they sounded so arrogant, so presumptuous on her part. She wanted to take them back.

Yet to her surprise, Tory simply came up behind her and kissed her neck.

"I almost didn't," he said and walked out of the kitchen.

Isobel was too stunned to reply.

IN THE bathroom, Tory looked down at his hand, now covered in a thin layer of dry, crusty toothpaste. The analytical side of him told him this was a stupid practice based on the lack of medical knowledge. He needed medicine, a salve, something besides this …ignorance. Okay, yes, he talked to Ashley about natural remedies, but there was a difference between what nature had to offer and what was found lying around the house. Really, had he recommended something like this to her, then he would've been no better than the quacks of yore who sold snake oil to unsuspecting peasants.

However, despite all his disbelief, Tory had to admit the toothpaste was working. The pain had subsided. He had no doubt that once he washed his hand, the skin would not show any signs of the burn.

Hell of a way to start the morning, he thought. All he wanted to do was make breakfast for Isobel. How was he to know he was so inept in the kitchen? All the cooking he had done in the last four years was done in the microwave.

Perhaps that should have been a clue.

I should have stuck to toaster waffles and coffee.

Tory washed his hand, checked the skin and confirmed what he knew: he was fine. Isobel was right. He chuckled at the confidence with which she treated him. And he was the doctor.

Then he recalled the feel of her skin on his lips. The smell of jasmine on her. It amazed him that at that moment he didn't have to think about kissing her, he just did it. It came naturally to him, like it used to when they were first married. He didn't have to ask for permission, he just did it. He loved it. He loved that she was there with him right now, loved the effect she was having on him, physically and emotionally.

Back in the kitchen, Tory was surprised to find it clean.

"Why'd you clean up?" he asked her with disappointment.

"Because it was dirty and your hand was hurt," she said as she poured coffee into a mug.

He held his hand up to show he was fine. She smirked and held her head up assertively. *No, arrogantly, definitely arrogantly,* he thought.

"I was fixing breakfast for you," he sulked, taking a seat at the counter. He wanted to do something for her for a change.

She came over with the coffee and slid it in front of him. With a smile on her face, she said, "That's sweet, but you didn't have to."

Tory met her gaze and took a deep breath, jasmine filling his lungs. She licked her plump lips as her beautiful brown eyes stared back at him. Did she know how alluring she was at that moment? What would she do if he kissed her again, only this time on the lips, full and hard? Would she respond to him? Would she wrap her arms around his neck and press her breasts against his chest? Let him take her…

"Tory?"

His face grew warm when he realized he was fantasizing about her while she was waiting on him to respond. And he was, just not the way she was expecting.

Get a hold of yourself, he thought, then cleared his throat. He adjusted himself as discreetly as possible, the heat from his body raising the temperature in the room.

"So, we go out then," he said.

"I could fix something really quick," she offered.

"Just get dressed," he insisted.

She didn't say another word and did as he asked. Tory exhaled the breath he had been holding in. He felt like a teenager again.

FOLLOWING A pleasant brunch that ran into the lunchtime crowd, Tory and Isobel took a walk. Then they went to see a movie. He let her pick, not really caring about the selection. Truthfully, he just wanted her to enjoy herself. He paid for the tickets and popcorn and led her to into the dark theater to watch the film. However, after a few minutes, it became apparent to Tory that *he* wasn't going to be appreciating any of it. He couldn't concentrate on anything but Isobel, especially when she shifted in her seat and moved closer to him. Her arm touched his and it felt like electricity moving through him. He had been with a few other women besides Isobel, but he could scarcely remember feeling anything like this with them. It was like his body was coming back to life.

Good thing it's dark in here, he thought, adjusting himself again. It seemed that's all he had been doing that day. He leaned in the opposite direction and impatiently waited for the end of the film.

"Let's get something to eat," Isobel suggested as they left the theater. "We could go to that restaurant your dad took me to. I think you'll like it."

"Sure," he muttered, though he wasn't feeling hungry.

Well, not for food…

It was dark by the time they returned home. Isobel smiled so hard and so often, it made Tory's cheeks hurt. She enjoyed their day, and that's what counted. He wanted to see her happy, to see her safe and cared for. And she was. All that and more. She possessed the other part of him that he was missing; and as the day came to a close, Tory decided he wanted to feel whole again.

Inside the apartment, Tory locked the door as Isobel reached for the overhead light.

"Leave it off," he said, dropping his keys on the counter.

She turned around, a puzzled expression on her face.

"Why?"

With his heart beating hard but sure, Tory approached her, placed his hand on the nape of her neck, and pressed his lips to hers. He rested his other hand on the small of her back and pulled her close to him. Isobel remained stiff, surprised and unsure, but as he continued to kiss her, she relaxed and melted into him. She felt warm and soft against his body, just like he knew she would.

He opened his mouth and let his tongue seek hers, dancing together as they made contact. Tory let his hands roam her body, touching and kneading the flesh that had been denied him for too long. He pushed her back against the wall and deepened the kiss. In that moment, an indescribable need for Isobel filled him and created in him a desperation to make her his again.

Tory swept her into his arms and carried her to the bedroom, unable to think of anything except how good she felt. He laid her down on the bed and settled over her, still kissing her. He made quick work of removing his pants, while she removed hers. Then he pushed her legs open and thrust into her. The air gushed from his lungs and he stopped, suddenly surrounded by her warmth. He was vaguely aware of Isobel's hands cupping his face, her voice gently urging him on. Tory rocked back and forth on his knees, drawing moans from Isobel with each lunge forward.

Unfortunately, their time apart had been too long, and Tory didn't last. Within minutes, he gave into the need to let go and fell over the proverbial cliff into Isobel's waiting arms. She held him close as he spilled his seed into her, expelling every last bit of energy he possessed. When he finished, Tory buried his face in the crook of her neck and held onto her.

He had found heaven and he never wanted to let go.

It was only after he caught his breath that Tory thought about the brevity of the act. Self-conscious and just a little embarrassed, he lifted his head and quipped, "Well, that went a lot quicker than I remembered."

She chuckled and offered him an understanding smile.

With his heart so full it threatened to burst, Tory kissed her one more time. He lay back on the bed, pulling Isobel with him, and wrapped his arms around her, tucking her head against his chest, underneath his chin where he could breathe in her scent. Then he closed his eyes and was asleep within minutes.

Twenty

FOR THE SECOND DAY IN A ROW, Isobel woke later than usual. This time though, there was no guilt and no rush to get up. The bed was so comfortable; it was as if she was sleeping on a white, fluffy cloud that enveloped her and lulled her back to sleep. This felt nothing like her bed.

Her bed.

Oh God.

Isobel shot up. She wasn't in her bed; she was in Tory's. Alone. All the details of their evening tryst suddenly flooded her mind, their first joining as well as the second, a longer, richer experience, so unexpected and so…incredible. She lay back down and closed her eyes, remembering the urgency in his kisses, the passion in his touch, the control he willingly gave her.

Settling on Tory's pillow, Isobel took a deep breath and inhaled his scent. She enjoyed being with him, but what exactly did 'being with him' mean? Was it a lust-filled moment? A one-night stand? Payback for her actions? No, he wouldn't do that. But what if he was filled with regret now that the moment had passed? He left early, after all.

Granted he had to go to work, but she was the morning person, not him. He usually slept as late as possible before departing for work. Perhaps after coming down from the lustful high, Tory realized having sex with her was a mistake and he left so he didn't have to face her in the morning.

Don't be stupid. You're the one who did all the leaving.

Did this mean he wanted her to stay then? Tory was not the kiss-em-and-leave-em type; he didn't do one-night stands. Was this his way of saying he wanted her back?

The thought should have made her happy, but she could only groan as she rolled under the covers, fighting the urge to throw up. She hadn't told him about her pregnancy. She had been with him this long and hadn't said a word about the baby.

Why would she have, though? She never thought he would forgive her, much less take her back. Surely, she could understand that.

Oh, who was she kidding? She was never open to discussing the possibility of having children when she was with him. Now she was back, pregnant with another man's child. Tory would be livid. What was she going to do now?

ISOBEL GAZED at the clock. She had spent the day doing busy work—laundry, cleaning, filling out applications for housing assistance, anything to keep her mind off of that evening. Her fate would be decided when Tory came home.

Dramatic, aren't we?

What else could she be though? Where she ended up was contingent on him. She could hope, but right now, hope was a very dangerous thing.

It was about a quarter to seven when Tory came home. Ever the domestic goddess, Isobel was finishing up dinner when he walked in. He appeared tired, but oh so handsome. He was still in need of a haircut, but she had grown to love those dark, curly locks nestled on his head. The beard that he kept closely trimmed made him look so sexy. He was gorgeous.

"Hey," Tory said, a soft smile on his face.

"Hi," Isobel replied, as he placed his bag and keys on the counter. He approached her with quiet steps and glanced over her shoulder.

"What are you cooking?" he asked.

Isobel closed her eyes, taking in his distinctive scent.

"Spaghetti Bolognese."

"It smells good," Tory continued. He kissed her temple and added, "You smell good."

Before she could even think about responding, he left the kitchen for his bedroom. She understood the kiss didn't mean anything, but man, he knew how to get her heart going.

Isobel was plating the food near the stove when Tory came up behind her and wrapped his arms around her waist. He had changed and seemed more energized as he moved her hair back and nipped at her ear. Surprised at his brazenness, Isobel almost dropped the serving spoon she had in her hands.

"What are you doing?"

"Picking up where we left off last night."

Her heart pounded hard in her chest as Tory kissed her neck—short, sweet kisses that made the hair on her skin stand up. Any question she had about whether he felt any regret for last night was immediately answered.

"I've thought about you all day," he whispered as he loosened his grip and began caressing her hips, her belly and her breasts.

Words failed her as Isobel gasped at the pleasure he was offering her, pleasure she hadn't known in a long time. Tory slipped his hand beneath the elastic of her pants into her panties, causing Isobel to inhale sharply. All thoughts left her, and she gave in to the need to feel, to experience, to be loved. She dropped the spoon on the floor, then raised her arms up over her head to grant Tory better access to her. She ran her fingers through his hair and pulled him closer to her.

"God, you are so beautiful. I love your long, silky hair. And this gorgeous body of yours...you've gained weight in all the right places."

Stunned by his words, Isobel dragged herself out of his embrace and turned around.

"You're not supposed to say that!" she exclaimed.

"Why not?" Tory rebutted. "How much do you weigh now? One fifty? One sixty?"

"I'm not answering you!"

"Don't get offended," Tory said, in a playful tone. He closed the gap between them and lifted her chin so that she was looking at him. "You are by far the sexiest woman I know."

"What about Rebecca?" Isobel dared.

He didn't hesitate.

"She doesn't even compare to you."

Isobel looked into his green eyes and saw the truth of his words. He desired her and only her. Too aroused to argue anymore, she grabbed his t-shirt and pulled him to her so she could kiss him. She opened her mouth and invited him in. She wanted him to touch her and kiss her, to take her and fill her, to make her his again and again; and wrap her in the warmth and safety of his embrace.

Tory tugged her shirt off. Then her bra. Followed by her pants and underwear together. Unrestrained in his actions, he picked her up and set her on the nearly empty counter. He guided her onto her back and began caressing her body with his tongue. Isobel felt like a holiday meal, splayed out for him to enjoy. And enjoy he did, showering her with the attention she desperately craved from him. Further and further he traveled down her body until he reached her center of passion. She squirmed and cried out with each stroke; and eventually gave in to the euphoric sensation that came with surrender.

Satisfied, Isobel relaxed and tried to regain her breath. Tory gently kissed his way up to her mouth. By the time he reached her lips, Isobel could only smile—a dopey, foolish grin. She inhaled deeply and decided it was her turn to love on Tory.

Isobel held out her arm to him and he helped sit up. Then she pulled his shirt off, stepped down from the counter and finished undressing him. With a deep, passionate kiss, she coaxed him to the floor and straddled him, taking him deep into her body. Tory rewarded her with a groan and relinquished control to her. Desiring only to give him the same gratification he gave her, Isobel moved over him, slowly, provocatively, drawing out every sensation, touching every sensitive nerve. Over and over, until Tory could take no more. He released his seed with a cry. Isobel fell forward, her hands on the floor on either side of Tory's face and watched him until all heightened emotions had subsided. Gradually, he lifted his hands and pushed her hair back, cupping her face. They held each other's gaze, no words necessary to enhance the moment.

Well, Isobel could think of three, but she didn't dare speak them, not knowing if he would believe her or accept them.

Tory pulled her down and kissed her, slow and easy. Then he released her, smiled and said, "I'm hungry."

Isobel laughed.

Twenty-One

CHARLIE DROPPED HIS TRAY ON the table, the gravy from his mashed potatoes splattering everywhere. Tory glanced at him briefly before reaching for a napkin.

"And to what do I owe this?"

His friend sat down opposite of him, a casual expression on his face. Tory finished mopping up the mess and tossed the used napkins on Charlie's tray.

"Obviously I haven't been reaching you, judging by that stupid smirk on your face. So, I've decided to try something different."

Tory wouldn't have called his grin stupid, though it probably did look goofy from an outsider's perspective.

"And what's that? Spilling your lunch on me?"

Charlie ignored his comment.

"I'm giving you my blessing. You have my permission to sleep with Isobel and do whatever the hell you want to do."

Tory stopped eating.

"So, we're trying reverse psychology now?"

Charlie grabbed his spoon and dug into his food. He shrugged his shoulders and said,

"No, man. Obviously, you care about this girl to stick with her this long after she did what she did. I mean, I've never had anything against Isobel specifically, except, you know, that whole abandonment thing; and well, the fact that she probably ran around like a skank for four years. Other than that, if she makes you happy, then you have my support."

Insults aside, Charlie was being sincere. The words stunned Tory silent. Now he was really confused. Tory fixed his eyes on his friend, trying to read him or at least get an inclination as to what was going on in his head. The man had always been steadfast in his convictions—except when a girl was involved.

"So, what's her name?" Tory asked.

Charlie smiled.

"You remember Jess, the nurse in radiology? We went out last night."

Tory laughed.

"And?"

"And…she's fantastic."

"Aww," Tory teased. "You're in love."

Charlie pitched his napkin at him.

"I'm joking. That's great," Tory said.

"Now I can look as goofy as you do."

"Whatever. When are you going to see her again?"

"Tonight. We're going to some play or something. I don't know. I let her pick."

"Did you get the tickets?"

"Not yet."

"Good luck with that then."

"Maybe we'll just skip the play and go back to my place for a home-cooked meal."

Tory snorted.

"What are you going to do, boil her a hot dog?"

"Like you can do any better."

"I don't have to. I've got Isobel."

"And the truth comes out, ladies and gentlemen. You're just keeping her around to cook for you."

"Don't hate, man."

"I'm not. Just calling it like I see it."

Before Tory could respond, they were interrupted.

"Hey boys."

Only one person he knew addressed them like that: his dad. Tory turned around to see his father approaching their table.

"Hey Dad," he said.

"Mr. Jamison," Charlie acknowledged, then cleared his throat. "Tory, I gotta run. I'll talk to you later." He picked up his tray and wove through the maze of tables without a glance back.

"Why does he always act like that around me?" Henry asked, filling Charlie's vacated seat.

"It's not you. He's afraid of Mom. Figures when you're around, she's not too far behind," Tory explained as he dove back into his food.

His father chuckled.

"She wouldn't hurt a fly."

Tory snorted.

"I'm glad you think so," he said, recalling how she treated Isobel. "What brings you here today?"

"Your mom is lecturing the first-year residents. I tagged along to see you." Since retiring a year earlier, Tory's dad traveled with his mother, who often spoke at conferences or lectured in classrooms. He was immensely proud of her and doted on her whenever he got a chance. "So, how're things going?"

"Fine," Tory replied, knowing where the conversation was headed.

"How's the job?"

"Fine."

"When are you going to call your mother?"

"Dad, please don't."

It'd been over a month since he last spoke to his mom, over a month since he threw her out of his apartment. It wasn't a proud moment for Tory, but she didn't leave him much choice. Now that he was on the other side of it, he felt even stronger about his decision. If she couldn't accept Isobel, couldn't accept his decision to help Isobel, then there was little they had to talk about.

"You're her only child."

"I'm yours too and you don't harass me. Why can't she just accept that I'm a grown man who can take care of himself and make his own decisions?"

"Because she's your mom."

Tory sighed and sat back in his chair, dropping his spoon and napkin onto the tray. This was the same argument his father always gave him, followed by the obligatory 'you'll understand one day' statement. He was tired of it. He loved his parents immensely, but he was his own man.

"And because you're so much like her," his father added.

"That makes no sense."

"You're hard-headed, just like her; and neither of you are willing to concede a fight first. You've always been like that. At some point though, one of you is going to have to be the bigger person and talk to the other."

"She can be the bigger person."

Henry shook his head.

"Son, when you get to be our age, you tend to be stuck in your ways, making change difficult. One day you'll understand; right now, though, I need for you to reach out to her. She's your mother. She loves you and she's only looking out for your best interests."

"By kicking Isobel out?"

"By protecting you. I'm not defending her actions, just suggesting maybe you see it from her point of view."

Tory sighed. He hated disappointing his dad. The man was soft-spoken and gentle, but he was stronger than anyone else he knew. He had to be to deal with Sarah Jamison on a daily basis. And for that reason alone, Tory agreed.

"I'll call her," he finally said.

"Great," his dad exclaimed. Standing up, he walked over to Tory and kissed him on the temple. "I've gotta get back. Thank you for doing this for me."

Tory nodded his response.

Henry started past him but stopped and turned back.

"Oh, and it looks like you've put on a few pounds. I'm glad she's taking care of you."

Tory shook his head in disbelief as his father walked off. That his parents could be so different and still function as one unit was amazing. Here he hadn't talked to his mother in weeks and she was content to make assumptions about his life, while his father seemed to understand and accept his personal life without delving into it.

And yes, Isobel was taking care of him. She had once told him that the Spanish word for well-cared-for was *querida*. It indicated a person who carried extra weight was beloved because of the time it took to make meals and sit and share it with them. The concept was simple and profound; and now that he and Isobel were intimate again, he couldn't help but consider how lucky he was to go home to her in the evenings. How he ever lived without Isobel, he didn't know.

Lately, though, that's what had him worried: he was getting too attached to her while they had yet to discuss what the future between them might be. Was there even a future to talk about? Her behavior towards him hadn't changed with this new development in their relationship. She was still quiet, still reserved, though quite responsive in the bedroom. Was it possible she felt for him what he felt for her, or she was she only just showing her gratitude?

The very thought made Tory sick. As much as he enjoyed her, he didn't want her responding to him out of obligation. But the fact was he didn't know what was going on in her head. He didn't know how she felt or even if he wanted to know. The old fear that she would leave him was popping up more and more lately, robbing him of his voice. He could simply ask, or sit her down and talk to her, but if he didn't say anything, he wouldn't know the truth, especially if the truth was something he didn't want to hear.

Okay, so that approach was highly naïve, but he wasn't ready to face the alternative, the worst-case scenario just yet, the chance she would reject him.

Again.

Maybe his mother was right: maybe he did need help making decisions.

THE BELL above the door chimed. Instantly the scent of fresh baked goods impinged itself upon Tory. *Pan dulces, pastelles, tortas.* His mouth watered as a huge glass case with these treats filled his sights and made him hungry.

"Can I help you?" a short, hardy Latina asked from behind the case.

"Actually, I'm here for Isobel," he answered, tempted to add an order of sweets to that.

She arched an eyebrow.

"And you're?"

"Her husband," he replied.

The woman smiled and stepped around the counter. She wiped her hand on the apron and offered it to him.

"She's spoken a lot about you. I'm Karen."

He shook her hand.

"Tory," he stated, wondering what Isobel had said.

"She's upstairs. We're about to close the *panaderia*. If you give me a moment, I'll get her."

"Thanks."

Karen returned behind the counter.

"So, you're a doctor," she asked.

"A pediatrician."

"A wonderful job, I'm sure. You see children at their worst and help them feel better."

Tory smiled.

"That's a great way of looking at it."

"I admire anyone who works with kids. It takes a lot of patience. I raised five by myself, so I know what I'm talking about," Karen continued as she closed out the register. Tory thought to comment, but she continued talking. "I'm a grandmother now. Six beautiful grandkids. And I'll tell you, I spoil them rotten, feed them all the *pan dulce* they want before sending them home. But that's my reward for all the heartaches I went through as a mother. It takes patience."

Isobel had described how friendly her boss was. Tory was surprised however at the ease with which she spoke to him, like they had known each other for some time.

Karen grabbed her things and moved to the doorway leading to the back of the bakery.

"It was nice meeting you, Dr. Tory," she said with a nod. Before she disappeared, she offered him a mysterious smile and added, "Be sure to ask Isobel about her good news when she comes downstairs."

Tory's heart skipped a beat. There were few times women used those words and they were usually associated with babies. He was excited for a moment as he considered the possibilities, but he had to compose himself. He had only been sleeping with Isobel for a week. There would be no good news...at least, not yet.

The lust in him made no consideration for protection when he had sex with Isobel. She had been on the pill in the past but given her situation now he doubted she was using it. And since pregnancy was hardly a concern to him, he didn't push for birth control. Perhaps it was no issue for her either, since she made no effort to prevent pregnancy. However, the fact that she was gone for four years should have been a motivator for him to get some form of prophylactic. Who knew what kind of disease…?

God, now you sound like Mom, he chastised himself, glancing around as if others could hear the conversation. *Surely if Isobel had contracted something, she would have told you.*

She might not know. You're the doctor; you know how these things work.

Yes, he knew, and he knew better. Which meant he needed to talk to Isobel, but how was he supposed to start that conversation?

Excuse me, Isobel, do you have any venereal diseases that you know of, or any reason to suspect you might?

Ugh! Why did their relationship have to be so complicated?

"Tory!"

He turned at the mention of his name to see Isobel standing at the doorway Karen had exited by. Her hair was pinned back, and her dress dusted with flour. She looked as radiant as she did messy. He couldn't help but smile.

"Hey."

"What're you doing here?" she asked moving towards him.

"I was off early; thought I'd swing by and pick you up."

She smiled appreciatively at him, then kissed his cheek.

"Let me grab my things."

She was back within minutes. They left the *panaderia*, but instead of heading home, Tory turned in the opposite direction.

"Where are we going?" Isobel asked.

"Out to eat. You hungry?"

"Yeah," she replied.

There was a line of customers waiting to be seated when they arrived at the restaurant. After giving their names to the hostess, Tory led Isobel to a vacant corner of the lobby. She stood close to him, gazing at the painting on the wall. She seemed lost in her own thoughts, and he wondered what was going through her mind. Did she wonder, like he did, what was in their future? Or was she just enjoying the moment? He probably needed to do the same. After all, he had a beautiful Latina standing next to him, who happened to be incredible in bed; whose body was perfect, whose big, brown eyes bored a hole into his soul every time she looked at him, whose sexual appeal had increased one-hundred-fold since they married and whose love he craved.

With a sigh, Tory tried to come up of something to say that would distract him from his thoughts.

"I met Karen," he finally said. A safe-enough topic.

Isobel turned to face him, her hands resting on his chest. Instinctively, he placed his arms around her.

"She mentioned you two had talked."

"I think she would have pulled out the family photos had we hung around long enough."

She chuckled and agreed. "She's like that."

Tory then remembered what the woman said. "She said to ask you about your good news."

Isobel's face lit up.

"Remember that conversation we had the other day about me belonging in the kitchen instead of an office? I talked to Karen about wanting to cook professionally and she's transitioning me to the kitchen. She's going to hire someone to replace me, then I'm going to start training with Mario, the head chef. I was in there today, helping out."

"That's wonderful," he said, hugging her. "I'm happy for you, Issie."

Without waiting for her to say anything, he kissed her. She returned his affection and responded to his touch with desire and eagerness, just as he had come to expect. Tory couldn't get enough.

Except they weren't at home.

Pulling away, Tory held her close nonetheless, breathing in her air, taking in her scent. He ran a finger down her cheek, following the curve of her chin.

"I should have good news more often," Isobel quipped.

Tory smiled, wishing they had other good news. Wouldn't that make the evening perfect? A child their love created…well, a child they created. He was sure of his love at least. Maybe this was something they could talk about tonight, something they could consider.

"Jamison, party of two!"

He kissed her lips once more, before taking her hand and following the hostess to their table. He pulled out her chair and helped her sit before taking his seat. When the waiter came by with their menus, he requested two glasses of champagne.

"We should celebrate," he said.

"You don't have to do that, Tory," she countered. "It's no big deal. It's just a job."

"Good news like yours doesn't come often enough."

She argued until the waiter returned with their drinks. Tory thanked him and raised his glass, ignoring her objections. Reluctantly, Isobel did the same. There was so much he wanted to say: how proud he was of her, of the person she'd become, of the ways she'd grown. How proud he was of what she had accomplished and what she was still to complete. How she remained true to herself in all this and how he still loved her. No, how he loved her more than he'd ever had and how much richer his life was because of her.

But no words came out. Not those anyway.

"To the future," was all he could manage before his doubts, his fears and his worries silenced him again. He drank his champagne, while Isobel set hers down; then they waited for their server to return.

Twenty-Two

ISOBEL STEPPED OUT OF THE shower and dried herself off. She approached the full-length mirror hanging on the back of the door and turned to her side to look at her growing baby bump. It wasn't very big; but as she ran her hand over her belly and let it rest there, she waited to see if she would feel the movement she felt the other day. It was subtle, but it set her heart aflutter with joy knowing what it was. She never considered herself the motherly type, but now she was anticipating every moment of the experience—the nine months, the birth, the breastfeeding, the first word, the first steps, the first tooth—all of it, except the part where she had to tell Tory she was pregnant. Isobel had yet to do so and with them continuing to sleep together, her time was running out.

But she didn't know how and after being silent this long, Tory would certainly think the worst—that she was trying to deceive him. Preparing for the worst-case scenario, Isobel continued searching for alternative living options. God knew she didn't want to lose him; but the truth was she might.

With a resigned sigh, Isobel got dressed. She needed to talk to someone, someone who would listen and not judge her, someone who would hear her and give her the advice she needed, someone who would be happy to get involved in her mess...

And I know who that is, she thought to herself. Pastor Martin. And so, after her monthly doctor's appointment, Isobel made her way to the church. Tory had given her use of his car, since it was his day off. She didn't want to borrow it, but because she had multiple stops to make, Isobel grudgingly agreed. Admittedly, she was spoiled by the rides Tory gave her in the past couple of weeks; the thought of spending all day on the bus was far from appealing. She wasn't above it of course; she just didn't care to do it today and given that she had to lie to Tory about where she was going, it was only appropriate she go to church.

Pastor Martin was all smiles when he saw her waiting in the church foyer.

"Isobel! It's so good to see you," he said, giving her a hug. Isobel was swallowed up in his embrace. "To what do I owe this visit?"

"Do you have a few minutes to talk? I need some advice," she said, far from meekly. She was there with a purpose and she sought to accomplish it.

The minister placed a hand on his chest and let his jaw drop.

"I am so honored you would come to me for advice."

Isobel rolled her eyes.

Pastor Martin laughed and led her to his office. He offered her something to drink, but she declined. Making himself comfortable in his desk chair, he turned to Isobel.

"So how things between you and Tory?"

Deciding to forego the obligatory 'beating-around-the-bush', Isobel answered honestly.

"We're sleeping together."

It must have been more than he was expecting from her, because his eyebrows arched, and his jaw dropped again. This time, though, the shock was real.

"Don't act so surprised. It's what you planned from the start," Isobel said.

It was another minute before the minister recovered. He smiled and feigned innocence.

"Whatever do you mean?"

She ignored him and continued.

"That's the reason why I'm here today."

Understandably, Pastor Martin looked confused, the direction of the conversation changing again. As honest as she had planned to be, Isobel found it difficult to tell him what she had yet to share with Tory. But she had to. It was that simple.

"I'm pregnant."

He still appeared confounded, unsure if he should be happy for her or not. She should have taken Nancy's advice and talked to him in the beginning.

"It's not Tory's."

As if she needed another reminder of this, her doctor gave it to her that morning: she was far enough along for her first full ultrasound. They would be able to see the baby next week and determine its sex, if she so desired. She and Tory hadn't been intimate long enough for that. She wanted to have a child with him, but she knew this wasn't the way he'd have it. She felt anxious with the guilt that consumed her. It wasn't fair to him, but it was the reality of the situation, a situation she couldn't change. She could change herself, she discovered, but not the mess she created.

Isobel looked to her pastor for some kind of answer, but he was speechless. She could see his mind racing with questions, trying to find a way to approach the dilemma she had brought him. After what seemed like an eternity and a day, Pastor Martin finally responded. With a sigh, he repeated her words, "It's not Tory's."

She shook her head.

"How far along are you?"

"Almost five months. I had an appointment earlier this morning."

"And I'm going to assume you haven't told Tory."

Isobel could only shake her head again.

Pastor Martin sat back and held her gaze.

"Alright. Talk to me."

And for the next thirty minutes, she did. Isobel told him about David and their sordid affair. She didn't spare a detail, her soul feeling lighter with each admission. There was still a weight there, undoubtedly because she had yet to tell Tory these same things, but she felt slightly better.

"Pastor, I never expected to stay with him this long. I never thought he would forgive me, much less take me back. I won't say I would've told him otherwise, but...I don't know. I might have. I might not. What I do know is that I want to stay. I've thought about what you said, that story you told me, and I want to be faithful. To Tory. To me. To this child." Her hand slid down to her belly. "It didn't ask to be born into this situation, any more than I did into mine, but it's my responsibility now to make sure it has the best life possible. I screwed up, I know that. But I won't let it suffer for my sins. I...I just don't know what to do right now and I don't want to lose Tory. Please, please, you have to tell me what to do."

Pastor Martin said nothing during her confession. He listened patiently, his expressions varying in degrees: anger when she described David's treatment of her, pain when she described their last meeting, joy when she told him about Tory's acceptance of her. And now…pride?

"Oh, Isobel," he said, smiling. He stood up and sat in the chair beside her. "You've grown so much. You always were a beautiful woman, but you were so unsure of yourself. Now though, to hear you speak with such love and selflessness…I am so proud of you."

Isobel couldn't stop the tears from flowing.

"I really wish I could fix yours and Tory's situation, but unfortunately, this is something you two will need to work out. You need to tell him, obviously sooner than later."

"I know," Isobel said, wiping her tears with her hand. "But I'm so scared he's going to tell me to go. I deserve it, I know, but I don't want to go anymore. I want to stay with him."

The minister reached over to his desk and retrieved a box of tissues. He pulled out a few and offered them to her. She wiped up her face and slumped in her seat, feeling hopeless.

"Did I ever finish that story about Hosea and Gomer?" he suddenly asked.

"They lived happily ever after," she half-heartedly replied.

"I suppose I left out some details, huh?" There was a tender smile on his face as he continued the tale he had begun over two months before. "Let's see. Oh yes, so Gomer had left Hosea with three teenagers, grounds for divorce on any day"—he let out a soft chuckle— "but he never stopped loving her. He couldn't. She was a part of him, despite the pain she had caused him. So, when he saw her in that marketplace years later, bound to a man whom he knew would never be able to love her the way he did, he couldn't help but yearn for her. Granted, he had to work through some forgiveness issues, but after seeing her, he knew there was no way he was going to let her go again. So, he got his checkbook, so to speak, went to the man's house, bought her debt and took her home.

"In the meantime, Gomer had to wait. Her happy ending was not dependent on Hosea; no, she had to learn to be faithful to herself, to be true to herself and therein be truly happy, but to find reprieve from her situation, to find the love she'd been missing, she had to wait on Hosea to rescue her, to get her out. I know it sounds sexist, but they were two halves of the same unit. She needed him in order to be whole.

"It's not easy to wait Isobel, but in this case, you don't have too many options. You're going to have to let Tory know the whole truth, everything you told me, and then you're going to have to wait on him to ask you to stay—that's the only way this can work. He may decide to send you away; if so, then you go with the knowledge that you are a strong and faithful woman. But considering all things, I do know Tory loves you. He wouldn't have taken you back into his bed so quickly if he didn't."

"Does he? Or is this just some way to get back at me?"

Isobel wasn't sure she believed it, but the thought had occurred to her more and more in the last week. Yes, Tory gave her body lots of attention, but he seemed so distant when they were together otherwise.

Pastor Martin didn't address her comment; he smiled at her instead. *Sadly,* she thought, then changed her mind: it was pity she saw on his face.

"I didn't tell you what the name Hosea means," he said.

Isobel shook her head.

"Salvation. His name means salvation. That's why she had to wait for him, because only he could save her."

TORY HUNG up his phone and sat down on his bed.

So much for spending the day in bed with Isobel, he thought. She was out running errands and now he had to go to the hospital.

Well, he didn't have to; he was choosing to. He had requested to know if Hannah was ever admitted and she had been earlier that morning. The little girl had a severe case of the flu: she was extremely dehydrated and feverish. Charlie was on-call when she was brought in and once he had begun treatment on her, he called Tory to advise him. Tory wasn't needed of course, but he wanted to be there for her and her mom. Ashley had her friends and family to lean on, but Tory had grown attached to them in the past year. They were, if he was honest enough to admit it, what his life should have been filled with. Now that Isobel was back, he supposed he needed to let them go, but not today and not now.

Tory grabbed some clean clothes and took a quick shower. After he was ready, he realized he had given Isobel use of his car, so he would have to take his bike. It would probably be faster, but after a few weeks of not using it, he had gotten lazy.

He left Isobel a note to let her know where he went and then headed out. He was a little tired when he got there, but no worse for wear. Tory made his way through the hospital to the pediatric floor, where Hannah was. There he found her, lying on a bed much too big for her, an IV attached to her little arm. Her expression was the most pitiful he had ever seen, but even as she met his gaze at the doorway, he could see that playful glint in her eye. She raised her free hand at him, offering half a smile. Ashley, who was seated beside her with her back to the door, turned around. When she saw him, she smiled too—a tired, relieved grin.

"Dr. Jamison," she said, standing up. "You didn't have to come."

He waved her back into her chair as he approached the bed.

"Sure, I did. I would've been wondering where Miss Hannah was when she didn't come in to see me this week."

Ashley shook her head, more embarrassed than anything else. She had confided in him early on that she worried she might lose Hannah because of all of her daughter's antics and maladies that resulted in doctor visits, but Tory assured her he wouldn't let that happen. He would be there as often as he could.

"How's my favorite patient?" Tory asked Hannah. He stood on the opposite side, brushing her hair back off her face. She giggled as she reached her arm up to touch his beard, still fascinated with the facial growth. She was too weak to keep her arm up though and soon dropped it to her side.

"She's doing better. She couldn't even keep sips of water down when I brought her in," Ashley replied.

Tory turned to her.

"How are *you* doing?"

"Unprepared. But what's new?"

Tory chuckled.

"I'm just ready to get home and get some sleep," Ashley continued. "My mom will be coming up to stay with Hannah after she gets off work and we'll just switch until Dr. Dyer releases missy here."

"Well, you're in good hands with Charlie. Is there anything I can get you?"

Before Ashley could respond, Hannah piped up and said, "Pizza!"

TORY VISITED with them for a while longer before leaving Hannah with a handful of lollipops and heading home. Relieved to know she was going to be fine, he looked forward spending the remainder of the day in bed with Isobel. He called home before he left the hospital, but there was no answer and Isobel didn't carry a cell phone. Now, as he entered his apartment and found the note he left where he left it, he could only wonder where she was. Running errands yes, but it'd be nice if she were home sometime soon. He couldn't wait to make love to her again.

Deciding he would wait for Isobel in bed, Tory stripped down to his boxers and slipped under the sheets. He chuckled to think he had actually made the bed up before his departure earlier. Isobel was definitely rubbing off on him, but then, it seemed she had rubbed off on everything in the apartment. Tory liked it. Though she still maintained her bedroom, her presence was especially noticeable in his. Her clothes were draped over the chair, her shoes were scattered about, and the sheets smelled of her. He took a deep breath and pictured her as he last saw her, beside him, naked and glowing, smiling and enjoying him as much as he was enjoying her. The very thought had him on fire with desire.

Too bad Isobel wasn't there. Tory offered to tag along with Isobel while she made her errands, but she insisted on going alone.

"At least take the car," he urged her, mainly so she could get back as soon as possible. If Isobel took the bus, then she would likely be gone all day. It was selfish of him, but he didn't want to spend one more minute without her. His fears aside, Tory knew it was time he talked to her. He needed to tell her how he was truly feeling—that he wanted to make her his wife again. He just needed to muster up the courage to say those words.

Tory grabbed the remote and aimlessly surfed through the channels. After the second time around, he finally settled on a talk show and half-heartedly listened to whatever they were talking about. His interest was minimal and when Isobel returned that afternoon, it was non-existent.

Without a word or greeting, Isobel walked through the kitchen and into her bedroom, her footsteps soft on the carpet. She lingered in there for a few minutes before appearing at the door of his bedroom. Tory laid back, his hands behind his head, and took in her lovely physique.

"Are you going to lie in bed all day?" she asked smiling at him.

"Only if you lie with me," he replied.

She was quiet for a moment, solemn even.

"Can we talk first?"

"We can do whatever you want."

Isobel pushed off the door frame and walked over to the bed. She stood at the edge of it, her large, brown eyes firmly on him. Tory climbed up onto his knees and moved towards her. He meant what he said, he'd do anything *she* desired but talking was the last thing *he* wanted to do now. She was radiant, and he couldn't help himself. Tory took her into his arms, spun her around onto the bed and settled above her. She squealed in delight and erupted into laughter.

"Tory!" she exclaimed.

"What? I'm listening," he said and kissed her mouth, hungry for a taste of her. They would certainly talk, but only after he had taken her again and made her cry out for him as she had done earlier that morning.

Not wanting to give Isobel the chance to argue again, Tory deepened the kiss. He felt his way down her body and caressed every inch beneath his hand. When he reached her belly, she placed her hands on his chest and gently pushed away from him. Unsure of her reaction, Tory stopped.

"What's wrong?"

Before she could respond the phone rang, the apartment phone, the one he rarely used and wasn't about to answer. He gazed at Isobel, still waiting for an answer.

"Aren't you going to get it?" she asked.

He shook his head.

"They can leave a message," he responded.

The phone rang again. Her eyebrows arched, as if questioning his decision. But he didn't move, at least until the answering machine picked up. Then he was especially glad he didn't as he heard the voice of his mother. He had called her yesterday, admittedly when he knew she would be out so he could at least say he did as his father asked. Tory wanted to talk to her, he just wasn't ready to do so—not yesterday and certainly not now with Isobel in his arms and the possibility of getting her out of her clothes increasing with every moment.

"You should talk to her," Isobel advised.

"I'll do that later," he said, nuzzling her neck.

"She's your mom," she insisted.

Tory almost said, *'and you're my wife,'* but he did not.

"She'll call back."

He nipped at her shoulder, kissing her through her shirt. Isobel closed her eyes and though she was still tense, she didn't stop him. Her hands relaxed as Tory inched down, covering her body with his. He pulled her shirt up and kissed the swell of breasts. Isobel moaned and gripped his shoulders with her hands. He stroked her stomach with his hands, caressing her body with his kisses. Tory pulled her pants off and moved between her legs. He laid his head on her belly and closed his eyes, inhaling her essence. He was content to hold her, relishing the fact that she was there with him, nothing to do but love each other all day.

"Tory, please, we need to talk...," she whispered, then stopped as her belly moved. Slight, but noticeable. Tory lifted his head when he felt Isobel tense up again. He would have made a crack about her being hungry or gassy, but for the look of worry on her face. He rose up onto his knees and looked down at her belly—her somewhat rounded belly.

Isobel sat up, extricating herself from under him. She pulled her shirt all the way down.

"Issie?"

Isobel backed up to the head of the bed, her eyes firm on her hands. She bent her knees up to cover her midsection completely. The look of guilt she bore cut him deeply.

"Isobel?"

Tory couldn't think, couldn't form two sentences to save his life. What was going on? Why was she acting like this?

Put it together, stupid. She's gained weight. She hasn't drunk any alcohol in the time she's been with you. This other guy is looking for her. She didn't want you with her this morning when she ran her errand…where did she go?

Confusion gave way to anger. He sat back on his legs, indignation rising. All this time she'd been with him, all this time she could've said something, all this time…

"When were you going to tell me?" he demanded.

Isobel lifted her head, her face already wet with tears.

"Tory, please, hear me out," she begged, but he refused to be moved. He had been wary from the start to take her in for this very reason. He knew this was where they would end up, with her betraying him, just as she did last time. Tory should have listened to what his mind was telling him.

"Hear what? What do you want me to hear? How you've been lying to me for over two months?"

Tory stood up off the bed and walked over to the wall to get away from her. He was so upset, his hands were shaking. How could he let this happen?

Isobel kneeled on the bed.

"Tory, please, it's not like that."

"So, you're not pregnant?" he snapped, turning back towards her.

She opened her mouth to speak but didn't immediately respond.

"I...I didn't tell you because I didn't want to hurt you—"

"You're gone four years! Not one damn word. Then you show up at my door, pregnant, and you didn't want to hurt me? You should have just stayed away."

Isobel stood up off the bed and walked over to where he stood. She reached out to him, but Tory pulled away from her.

"Please listen to me, okay?" she pleaded with him. "I made a mistake, I admit that. I made a mistake when I left, and I got into trouble. But I learned from my mistakes. I really did. I didn't tell you about this because I didn't expect you to ever forgive me. I didn't expect you to...take me back."

Tory shook his head and leaned back against the wall, marveling that just a few minutes earlier, he had been getting ready to make love to her. He didn't know whether he should laugh or punch the wall.

"I wanted it all, Isobel," he told her. "I wanted you back in my home and in my life. I fought everyone close to me who thought I was crazy for doing that. I even alienated my own mother for you. And this is what you do, play games."

"I'm not. I'm not playing games. I was going to tell you. Everything. Leaving was inexcusable, but I've changed. I'm not that woman anymore, Tory. I want to stay. I want to stay with you."

"For what? So, we can go on playing house and I can raise your bastard child for you?"

Isobel closed her mouth and let her shoulders slump, as shame filled her eyes. She seemed ready to shut down, just like she used to.

"You wouldn't even discuss having kids," Tory continued, seizing on her actions. "*You were scared, you'd be a horrible mom, you'd never bring a child into this screwed-up world.* Always an excuse, but never open to the idea. Then you whore yourself out and get pregnant by someone else."

Isobel hung her head as the tears continued to flow.

"All you ever did was use me," Tory pushed.

Isobel shook her head.

"That's not true," she said, her voice low, her eyes downcast. "That's not true."

"I was nothing to you except a distraction," he said. "And when that wasn't enough anymore, you left. Because that's what you do and that's who you are. You take and you take, and you think only of your-self!"

Isobel looked up then and met his gaze. Her countenance had changed. She was breathing hard and frowning, the emotion on her face mirroring his.

"That's not true, Tory, and you know it."

"I know that you lied to me for two months and now you expect me to take you back like nothing happened. All I ever did was love you. And all you ever did was take advantage of me."

Her nostrils flared and the frown on her face changed to anger. She clenched her fists and shook her head. Tory reared up to his full height, unwilling to be outdone by her rage. She had nothing on him. *He* was the one scorned again. *He* was the one who was betrayed by her duplicity. *He* was the victim, not her.

"You have no right to accuse me when *you're* the one holding back," she hissed.

"Excuse me?"

"You act so sanctimonious, talking about how you wanted it all, how you gave up so much. You're quick to play the victim here, but you're the one who used me!"

Tory opened his mouth to argue, but she cut him off.

"Why did you even let me stay if you were never going to forgive me? Was this your way of getting back at me? Did you feel entitled to my body after everything I put you through? I thought you were better than that, I thought you were better than…"

Isobel bit her lip, censoring herself, though the fire didn't leave her eyes. Tory jumped in, taking advantage of her silence.

"Better than your boyfriend?" he scoffed.

Isobel's mouth fell open and the color drained from her face.

"Yeah, I know about Harris," Tory said bitterly. "I know about the trouble you're in. I know all of that. Still, I thought maybe this time would be different with you. But you haven't changed. You're nothing but a selfish bitch. And I'm a fool for falling for you again when it's clear you never loved me."

The rage drained from Isobel's stance and her face softened up.

"I've always loved you, Tory."

Her words were like salt on an open wound and Tory couldn't stop himself: he smashed his fist into the wall behind Isobel. She recoiled from him and fell to her knees, her body curling up tightly as her hands covered her head. He would have never hit her, never, but it did him good to see her cowering on the floor like that. He wanted her to hurt like he was hurting, to know the pain she had brought him.

Isobel looked up, the fear in her eyes unmistakable. Even as satisfying as it was to see her like that though, Tory couldn't stop the ache in his heart.

"Just do what you do best and leave," he muttered; then grabbed the clothes he had strewn on the floor and left the room.

Twenty-Three

ONCE HE WAS DRESSED, TORY grabbed his keys and headed out. Still fuming, he drove around aimlessly, trying not to think. He couldn't deal with his situation right now; he didn't want to. He just drove around until evening came and he grew tired of driving.

Tory's stomach began growling. He needed food; he hadn't eaten all day. That he could fix. Settling on his usual place, Tory parked his car in a nearby lot and walked down the main street to the pub. Tory entered and went straight to the bar. Hardly the answer to his problems, but it seemed this was all he had been doing since Isobel returned. Maybe he should have taken it as a sign in the beginning. An omen.

The bartender approached him, placing a napkin in front of him.

"You look like you've had a rough day, honey. What can I get you?" she asked.

"Whiskey," he said, and requested a menu. After he ordered, Tory sat back and waited, his eyes on the television above the bar. He massaged his hand where he hit the wall and ignored all thoughts, except the ones that had to do with food and the game. He drank and he ate and that was his evening. He didn't move from the stool, even after he finished. Just cradled his drink in one hand and his head in the other. He was barely aware of the person now occupying the seat beside him.

"What can I get you?" the bartender asked.

"Just a soda, thanks."

Tory closed his eyes and sighed. It was Pastor Martin. Tory waited for the minister to clap his shoulder or say something, but the man didn't. He simply sat beside him. Tory lifted his head after a while and peered at the man of God. He was staring up at the game.

"What are you doing here?" Tory asked, his tone less than cordial.

"Just thought I'd catch a game."

Tory rolled his eyes.

"She called you?" he muttered.

Pastor Martin finally turned to him.

"Yes. She was worried about you."

Tory chortled, disgust filling him again.

"Worried about her meal-ticket is more like it."

"You don't believe that," the pastor said.

"Whatever."

Tory turned back to the television. He didn't feel like talking.

The bartender came back with Pastor Martin's drink.

"Let me know if you need anything else," she said and left them alone.

"Do you want to talk?" the minister asked.

Tory shook his head.

"I'm good, thanks."

Silence crowded itself between them, though the ambient sounds were loud and rowdy. Tory tried to go back to the indifference he had achieved before his pastor showed up, but it was too late—he was back in that room with Isobel, learning her secret, a secret she had kept from him for over two months. How could he not know she was pregnant? He was a doctor, for Christ sakes! He should have known!

Frowning, Tory sat up.

"I told you I wanted nothing to do with her. I told you I didn't want to be hurt again. But you had to get involved, didn't you? You had to push and invite yourself into a situation you had no business in." He paused and shook his head. "I loved her. She was all I thought about all those years, all I craved. But I was never enough for her." Tory picked up his shot glass but didn't drink. He placed it back on the bar and turned it round in his hand. "I'll admit I wasn't the perfect husband, but I tried. I didn't walk away when things got hard, I stayed. And for what? Then she came back, I spoke tenderly to her, just like you said. I thought we could return to the way things used to be, I thought we could try again, but apparently I was wrong."

"Did you tell her any of this?"

"For what? It wouldn't have changed the situation."

"Oh, I don't know. Sometimes we look for everything and everyone else to change not realizing the change needs to happen in us."

Tory groaned and dropped his head on the bar.

"God, now you're preaching."

"Look Tory, I didn't come here to preach at you, okay? And I'll be the first to agree with you: life sometimes sucks. It's never what we expect it to be. But we make the best of it. We confront the past and deal with the consequences."

Tory sat up.

"So, what, I'm supposed to accept this now? Deal with Isobel's indiscretion like nothing happened? And of course, because she's changed, I'm the bad guy if I put her out, I'm the ass if I say no, right? I never asked for any of this."

"No, you didn't. And I'm not suggesting you take her back. Yes, I involved myself in your affairs, but what happened between you and Isobel was a choice the two of you made. And now you two are going to have to decide what will happen from here. And if you can't decide, if you can't live with Isobel's mistakes, then you need to let her go."

The options seemed overwhelming at the moment, more than he could handle.

"What should I do?" Tory asked.

The answer came with no hesitation.

"Speak tenderly to her."

'Forgive her' was what Tory heard, and his mind spelled it out clearly: forgive Isobel and get to love her, or don't and live without her. He didn't have to approve of what she did; he just had to forgive. And this time, deal with the consequences. Deal with the past. The indiscretions. The baby.

A baby…was that so bad?

They sat in silence for a few minutes as Tory pondered the situation, pondered what he should do. His head began hurting and his stomach grew queasy. He resisted the urge to throw up and simply observed the minister as he drank his soda and watched the game, as if this was what he came to do. For a moment, Tory thought he saw the man smile as one of the teams scored.

"So that's it? No more advice? No stories?" Tory asked sarcastically, pushing his glass away.

Pastor Martin turned to him and smiled.

"Oh, I've always got advice; and stories too, if you want to hear them."

Tory shook his head and held up his hand.

"No, that's alright. I'm good."

"Let me just add this and I'm done. That story I told you? About Hosea and Gomer? I didn't tell you what the wife's name means. Completion. She was his other half, his missing half. He was empty without her because only she could complete him."

Tory didn't say anything. The words themselves seemed to sink in, but for a later time. He couldn't think about that now. He was definitely calmer than when he arrived, but he still didn't know what to do. And while he wasn't sure that he was ready to see Isobel, he knew it was time to go home. He started feeling around his pant pockets for his wallet, but Pastor Martin paid the bill before Tory could argue.

"Come on," he told Tory. "I'll take you home."

Tory shook his head.

"I drove."

"Which is exactly why I'm taking you home," the minister replied firmly. "We'll come back and get your car once you've sobered up."

Tory grudgingly agreed and followed him out into the parking lot. He wasn't staggering, but the ground did seem to be moving a lot. He was glad when he finally reached the minister's car. As he slid into the passenger seat, Tory decided he was finished with drinking. He was much too old to be acting like this, regardless of the situation that drove him to it. He rested his head against the cool glass and watched the scenery pass as Pastor Martin drove him home. It wasn't a long drive, and they soon pulled into Tory's parking spot at the apartment complex. He didn't look at the pastor as he said, "Thanks."

Pastor Martin nodded his head.

"We'll get you inside, then you can sleep this off. And I expect to see you at church this Sunday."

Tory rolled his eyes but didn't argue. It certainly wouldn't do him any harm to go to church. Look at the good it did Isobel since she came back.

Pastor Martin offered him a hand, but he exited the car on his own. Both traversed the path to his apartment, but even before they got to the front door, Tory could tell something was off. Ignoring the nausea and headache, Tory pulled his keys out and fumbled with the lock. He didn't utter a word to the pastor, just went in and walked back to his bedroom. The room was clean, and the bed was made up. He walked across the hall to the Isobel's room. It too was clean, just as she kept it—but all her things were gone. There wasn't a trace of her anywhere.

Isobel had left him. Again. This time though there was no mystery why; she was gone because of him. She was gone because he told her to go.

Twenty-Four

ISOBEL REMAINED STILL AS TORY grabbed his clothes and stormed out of the bedroom. She wanted to move, to get up off the floor and out of this stance of fear she had grown accustomed to, but her muscles were locked. Even with her arms shaking and her heart thundering in her chest, she couldn't move. All she could do was entertain the questions that were now demanding answers: how did Tory know about David? How long had he known about him? And why did he let her get close again?

None of that really mattered, though. She had no one to blame but herself for the way things transpired. She should have told Tory sooner, should have mentioned her condition at the change in relationship, should have…

The front door slammed shut. Tory was gone.

Isobel dropped her head into her hands and finished crying her tears. She tried holding them back earlier, as Tory spewed his comments at her, but they would not be contained, then or now. Drop by drop, stream by stream, until she had nothing left but a headache. She laid down where she was and closed her eyes, wishing things had gone differently—but just wishing, because it was too late to hope.

How long she lay on the floor, Isobel didn't know. She pulled herself up into a sitting position and looked around the room. Her shoes were in the corner, her clothes on the chair; everything carelessly tossed aside after Tory brought her into his bedroom to make love to her last night. The caress of his kisses, the love in his touch, all of that had been replaced with angry words and hurtful gestures this afternoon. She hurt him again and for the briefest of moments Isobel considered leaving. It was what he wanted, after all.

No, they were words spoken in anger, she reminded herself, pushing aside all thoughts of escape. Yes, she hurt him, but she was going nowhere until they talked. Until he told her he didn't love her and didn't want her there. Until he gave her divorce papers. It was probably arrogant on her part, on some level, but he did say he wanted her back...or something like that anyway. Maybe if he had a chance to calm down and was willing to forgive her...

Isobel sighed. Yes, it was arrogance, but she was done running. If Tory did in fact want her to leave, she would go and never look back, but he would have to make it official and end their marriage. No more avoidance and no more games.

Isobel stood up and slowly moved to the bed, her body aching and hurting. She had laid on the floor too long. She thought of the way she reacted to Tory. He would have never hit her, she knew that, but she couldn't stop herself from flying back and protecting herself the way she did. It had become inherent and she prayed it was something that would dissipate with time.

The silence in the apartment was deafening. Isobel busied herself with cleaning up the room and getting dressed. Still Tory remained gone. She told herself he needed time to adjust, to think everything through, but the longer he stayed gone, the more she worried. What was he doing? Was he out with Charlie? Was he drinking? He was driving; surely he wouldn't drink and drive, would he?

Upset by the thought, Isobel grabbed the phone and called Pastor Martin. She sighed with relief when he answered on the second ring.

"Pastor, it's me, Isobel," she stated, unable to still her voice.

"What's wrong?"

Isobel explained what happened, choking back tears as she relived the moment.

"Do you want me to go over there?" the minister asked.

"No. I'm just worried about Tory. I don't know where he went."

Pastor Martin was silent for a moment before he said, "I've got an idea. I'll go find him."

Isobel felt a weight lift off her heart. At least Tory would be safe. She thanked her pastor and hung up. With nothing left to do but wait, she decided to shower up before getting something to eat. Even as hungry as she was, she wouldn't have been able to keep anything down right then. She needed to calm down herself. She grabbed a change of clothes and tried to relax under the streams of hot water. It did her muscles good, but not her heart. She couldn't get it to stop racing and figured it was something she would have to deal with until Tory got home.

If he comes home.

Ignoring the thought, Isobel dried herself off and got dressed. She was brushing her hair when she heard the front door shut. The trembling in her hands returned. She shut her eyes and swallowed hard, willing herself to calm down. This was what she wanted, for Tory to come home. Now she would say everything she had been practicing; and if need be, she'd pack and go.

With the momentary surge of courage, Isobel stepped out of the bathroom.

"Isobel."

She froze as panic seized her heart. It was David, standing in Tory's hallway, calling her name.

"Isobel."

She was too shocked to initially respond. But her body seemed to know what to do instinctively: she backed up until she hit a wall. She needed to get away from him.

"What are you doing here?" she asked.

"I should ask you the same thing," he said, his tone casual. He moved closer to her, his hands extended out towards her. "I've been looking for you for months."

She detected no anger, but he could swing from one end of the emotional spectrum to the other without notice. This made Isobel leery to reply: what could she say, how could she reason with him when it was obvious he was not being reasonable at the moment, not if he had broken into Tory's apartment.

"Isobel, aren't you glad to see me?"

She cautiously edged along the wall to her bedroom, praying Pastor Martin had found Tory and was bringing him home now.

"When you left and didn't come back, I didn't know what to do. You had me so worried. I looked everywhere I knew to look for you. You didn't give me much to go on, so I had to do some searching. I had to find you." David moved closer to her, making her more and more nervous as she considered what he would do if—and when—he caught her. "People kept telling me no, but I knew I'd find you. And I finally did. And I want you to know I forgive you for what you did to me. I just want you to come home."

Isobel glanced at his neck; there was a faint scar in the same area she cut him in. She could only imagine the rage he felt after she'd gone. Was he harboring it now? He said he'd forgiven her.

The irony struck her in that moment: the man she wanted forgiveness from was holding back, while the man she wanted to get away from was offering it to her freely.

"Isobel, I love you."

She thought about all the times he had hit and kicked her. All the times he had made her afraid. All the times he had threatened her. She knew better than to argue, but she just couldn't contain herself—not when she had finally learned what love was.

"You don't love me," she returned as she reached the door to her bedroom. "You don't know what love is."

David frowned.

"I love you," he insisted.

Hearing the resolve in his voice frightened her and in a desperate attempt to get away from him, Isobel turned around and grabbed the doorknob. But it only slipped through her fingers as David grabbed her hair in a tight fist and pulled her back towards him. She screamed, pain surging through her neck and back. She reached up and tried to push him off, but he was too strong for her. He wrapped his arm around her and tugged her body back towards him. With ease, he pulled her up off her feet so that his face was nuzzling hers.

"Don't you know how much I've missed you?" he asked, all softness gone from his voice.

"David, please don't do this," she begged.

"All I wanted was a chance to apologize and make it up to you," he said, dragging her back towards the living room. "I need you, Isobel. In my life. It's not complete without you. I know I've hurt you, but I'll do better. I'll be better. You make me a better man."

Isobel held onto his wrist and struggled against him.

"Please, baby. I need you to come back with me. I just want to love you."

"Let me go," she pleaded.

"Tell me that you love me. Tell me you'll go with me."

"David, let me go. Please."

He tightened his hold on her arms.

"Tell me you'll go with me." His tone changed to threatening.

"Please, David. I don't want to go…"

He let her go and pushed her up against the wall, her head hitting it hard. He hovered over her, his hand still gripping her hair tightly, his face scrunched up in anger.

"Is it because of him?"

"David—"

"Is it?" he yelled.

Isobel flinched at his raised tone, throwing her hands up to his chest.

"No! No!"

"He doesn't love you like I do. He tried to keep me from you, but I found you anyway. That should show you how much I want you, how much we're meant to be together."

Isobel couldn't stop the tears streaming down her face. Even still, she had to find a way to get away from David. He was too strong for her to fight and she couldn't reason with him; perhaps if she could get to a phone, call someone, then maybe she could get to safety.

"Okay," she whispered. It was all she could manage.

He seemed surprised by her acquiescence.

"Okay?" he repeated.

"Okay. I'll go with you."

He took her hands in his and squeezed them.

"You'll see. I'll make you happy. I'll love you the way you were meant to be loved."

David kissed her on the mouth. Isobel did all she could do not to push him away from her.

"I have to get my things," she said, and pulled her hands out of his.

"I'll help you."

She stopped.

"I'll get it, David."

"No, we'll get them."

He took hold of her hand again, a hard look on his face. He wasn't going to allow her out of his sight—ever. Subjugated once again, Isobel stifled the sob that threatened to come out and lead the way to her bedroom. Maybe if she had talked to Tory, if she had only told him about the baby, she wouldn't be in this mess. But to think like that was useless. Even if Tory still wanted her, it didn't matter anymore. He would come home to find she was gone...just as he had told her to do, just as she had done in the past.

Twenty-Five

TORY SANK DOWN ON THE BED and ran his hands through his hair. Even though he had been home for only a minute or so, an overwhelming loneliness enveloped him. Everything felt wrong. Everything *was* wrong. His breathing became shallow and his heart sank down into his gut. He was lost, and he had no one to blame but himself. He had told Isobel to go, he had pushed her away even though she wanted to stay.

He considered the words he spewed at her, the anger that laced his voice, the fear he instilled in her. Maybe he was within his right to be upset with her, but he was out of line behaving the way he did. And not just today. He had treated the woman he loved with disregard, ignored her, let her pick up after him, cook for him, care for him, all while he was ungrateful and rude, not once offering forgiveness, not once offering an apology for his behavior, not even when their relationship changed. Whatever she had once been, Isobel had changed and did not deserve his treatment of her.

The nausea returned as did his headache. Now he really did want to throw up.

There were footsteps in the hall. Tory looked up to see his pastor. The man wore a solemn expression on his face.

"She's gone," Tory quietly said. "She wanted to stay, and I told her to go."

"I'm sorry," Pastor Martin offered; then paused briefly before asking, "What are you going to do?

Tory didn't know what to say. After the way he acted, he couldn't expect her to forgive him if he went after her. He was the one who needed to change as she had.

Something like bile rose up in his esophagus. Except it wasn't bile. It was something else, something worse.

If Isobel did change, she wouldn't have reacted the way she used to, she wouldn't have left.

But she did.

But she wanted to stay. She sent Pastor after you because she was worried about you. She fought you earlier, instead of clamming up. She stood up to you. She wouldn't have done any of that if she hadn't changed…right?

Then where is she?

He scratched the stubble on his chin. What wasn't he getting?

"Tory?"

He turned to Pastor Martin, whose expression had gone from expectancy to full of pity. Tory knew he was a pathetic sight. He wondered for a moment if that's how the pastor beheld Isobel when she returned. Did he give her the same advice, tell her the same stories? What advice would he offer now? Would he tell her to speak tenderly to…him? To treat him humanly, remember what their love was, see him as someone worth cherishing, someone to be taken care of, someone to be forgiven?

The thought made him chuckle. He couldn't picture Isobel struggling as he had. Some things, like caring, came naturally. And the rest? Well, somewhere in the last four years she picked up the temperament to deal with difficult...

The last four years… The trouble Isobel got in… The bruises on her body that morning after her arrival; green, purple and yellow, discoloring her beautiful skin… The boyfriend, who was still looking for her…

"Oh God," Tory uttered as he rose to his feet. Cursing himself, he pushed past the pastor and went to the kitchen. He grabbed the phone and pulled out the card the detective had given him. He called the mobile number listed, but it had been disconnected.

Pastor Martin joined him in the kitchen.

"What's going on?"

Dialing the number for Dr. Hall, Tory stated, "She didn't leave voluntarily."

"What are you talking about?"

"Her...ex," Tory uttered with disgust. The words left a bitter taste in his mouth, but now wasn't the time for that. "He's been looking for her, at the hospital, I guess thinking she would come back to me. I should have done more, I should have said something to her, but I didn't. I was too stupid, too jealous..."

Dr. Hall picked up the line.

"Hello."

Tory turned his attention to the phone.

"Dr. Hall, it's Tory. I'm sorry to be calling you late, but I need to ask you something."

"It's alright, Tory. What is it?" the man replied. Obviously, he could hear the urgency in Tory's voice.

"The officer who was asking for Isobel, has he been back?"

"Yes, yesterday in fact. He spoke with one of the nurses in the family clinic. I called security and had him escorted out."

"Do you know what they talked about?"

With a sigh, Dr. Hall said, "Tory, you know she's pregnant, right? She's been seen at the clinic a few times now."

If Tory wanted any further confirmation that she was expecting, this was it.

"Yeah, I know."

There was a slight pause before the other doctor continued. "Is everything okay?"

"Honestly, I don't know," he sighed. "But I appreciate your time. Thank you."

"Let me know if I can help."

"I will." And Tory hung up.

Without wasting another breath, he dialed 9-1-1. He didn't understand the situation, nor could he drive away the doubt that accused him of jumping to conclusions; he simply knew he couldn't lose Isobel again, not like this.

Pastor Martin remained with him, keeping a silent vigil in the background as the emergency dispatcher took his information. The man on the other side of the line promised an officer would be along shortly. And indeed, within minutes, a couple of police cars had arrived. Two officers approached his doorstep. To his surprise, one was Rebecca—tall, beautiful Rebecca, with long, blonde hair and lovely, blue eyes. Tory couldn't help but appreciate her features, but the attraction was gone now. He knew it had been fleeting, but he didn't realize how wholehearted his attention to Isobel was until now. Rebecca was right: only Isobel held his heart. Only Isobel made him whole.

"I heard the call on the radio. What happened?" she said. Worry was etched into her face, concern mixed into her voice. For him. After all this time.

"My wife's been kidnapped," he stated simply; and knew by the look on her face he needed to explain. Not just for the police report, but for the relationship they once had. For the first time since he met her, Tory was completely honest with her. He told her about Isobel, about her leaving and her return and how they were still married. He walked her through the apartment and shared his concerns, hoping she would understand his fears and his regrets, hoping they could hear the urgency in his words.

This didn't appear to be the case though, when Rebecca turned to the other policeman and asked for a moment alone. Just as clearly as he saw the apprehension on her face when she walked in, he could see doubt written all over it now.

"I'll go take a look at the bedroom," the officer stated with a nod.

Rebecca waited until he was gone before she spoke.

"Tory, I appreciate your candor, but there's no evidence to back up your claim."

Tory wanted to scream. Why could no one see what he did?

"The man's been looking for her," he insisted, trying to keep annoyance out of his tone. He needed her to hear him. "He's hurt her before."

"That's a hefty accusation to make."

"I saw the bruises when she first came back. On her back, her legs."

"Did she tell you that's what they were from?"

"No."

"Then that's not enough."

"The way she reacted then. I, ah, got upset with her earlier and punched the wall." He couldn't help the shame from creeping into his voice. "She was more than scared; she was terrified, fearful. Isobel was never like that. It's a conditioned response. You and I have both seen it in our lines of work."

"Yes, and you and I both know that's still not enough."

He knew she was right, but he couldn't give up.

"Rebecca, please. I know I don't deserve your help, but I'm begging."

She held his gaze. He worried she had already decided to say no and was simply trying to find a way to do so without breaking his heart. But she didn't.

"Alright. Let me make a call."

She left the apartment and returned to her car. For the umpteenth time that evening, Tory felt lost. He dropped onto the couch, his head in his hands. Though he had sobered up—mostly—his head still hurt.

"Here."

Tory looked up to see Pastor Martin offering him a cup of coffee.

He thanked him and added, "You don't have to stay."

The cleric only shook his head as he took a seat across from him.

"I want to."

No other words were needed. The two men sat in silence as they waited for Rebecca to return. The other officer walked through the living room, making observations and asking questions. When he was satisfied, he advised he would return shortly and left Tory sitting, waiting. Each passing moment proved more difficult than the last when it came to being patient, but there was nothing else he could do until Rebecca returned.

When she did, Tory and Pastor Martin rose to their feet quickly. The grave expression on her face bothered him.

"I spoke with my captain," she said. "Apparently Harris was suspended about a month back, pending an investigation into a lawsuit that states he allegedly roughed up several detainees. Put one in the hospital." Rebecca must have seen the worry on his face, because she quickly added, "Tory, wait. That doesn't mean anything—"

"Doesn't it?" he spewed angrily. Why could no one else see this? "If he roughed them up, then it's likely he did the same to Isobel. He's been looking for her since she left, sniffing around the hospital because of me, trying to get her back. I know there's no evidence for it, but he's got her. I'm certain of it. She wouldn't just have left—"

"Tory, stop. Listen." She reached out and touched his arm, gently applying pressure in an attempt to calm him. "I was going to say, that doesn't mean anything, but given the circumstances, we're following up on this. We're going to talk to your neighbors, figure this out, okay?"

Tory searched her eyes, wanting desperately to believe her. Only when she moved closer to him and softened her grip to a comforting squeeze did he dare hope.

"Tory, we'll figure this out, okay?"

Unable to argue with her confidence, he nodded.

Twenty-Six

AS DAVID PLACED HER BAGS IN the trunk of his car, Isobel couldn't help but feel her last bit of hope dissipate into the darkness of the evening. He had helped her pack her things, then slip out of Tory's apartment as though she had never been there. And for what Tory would believe, she might as well have never come back.

David stepped into the vehicle and slammed the door shut.

"We'll stop and get something to eat and then we can get a hotel room before heading back in the morning. We've gotta take care of you now that you're carrying my baby," he continued.

Isobel closed her eyes as her arms flew instinctively over her belly. She hadn't told him, but he knew she was pregnant. Now his possessiveness over her would be complete. He would never leave her out of his sight. He would never let her go, and as they pulled out of the apartment complex, Isobel knew her freedom was forever gone.

They drove for the better part of an hour before stopping at a restaurant located off an exit ramp. It wasn't very busy, mostly travelers and tourist-types, where no one who would recognize them.

Since leaving the apartment, Isobel had uttered only a handful of words. Not that David noticed as he continued chatting away like a happy child who had finally received the toy he wanted. The way he was spontaneously filled with joy drew her to him in the beginning. It was infectious and she loved that. She loved the attention he gave her and thought for certain he could be the one to ground her. Admittedly though, she never loved him. Isobel thought she might eventually grow to but when that first hit came, it sealed the fate of their relationship and the day came when she left him too.

"Just two?" the hostess asked with a tired smile.

"Just two," David replied, his arm around Isobel's waist. Her skin crawled at his touch, but she couldn't push him off or she would risk his wrath.

"Follow me," the hostess said.

As they walked behind the woman, Isobel looked around at the faces of the other patrons. They were deep in conversation or food, no one paying them any attention. She was alone.

"Your server will be by in a moment to get your order," the hostess said before leaving them. David sat beside her, a smile on his face. He looked the menu over for a moment before turning his attention to her.

"I'm really glad you're in my life," he said.

Isobel said nothing in response. She focused on her menu, but found her appetite was gone by the time the waiter came. He was a polite, young man, no older than twenty, who seemed to be good with people going by the easy way he made conversation with David. When he turned to her to get her order, Isobel hesitated, unprepared.

"If you're not ready I could come back," he offered.

"Oh, uh, that would be great," she replied.

"I'll be back in a few minutes with the appetizer and if you're ready then, I'll get your order," the young man said.

"Thanks."

When he left, Isobel turned back to the menu.

"You need to eat, Isobel," David said, his voice filled with concern.

"I know," she said softly.

"Something healthy for the baby," he added, perusing the menu for her. "A salad."

Her stomach turned and she felt as though she might throw up, but she didn't argue.

Or maybe she would.

"I'm not feeling well," she said, closing the menu.

"Are you sick?" he asked.

She shook her head.

"It's the pregnancy," she replied. "I'm going to go to the bathroom."

He stood up with her.

"I'll go with you."

"David, you can't go in the ladies' room."

"I want to make sure you're alright."

Though repulsed, she touched his hand and reassured him, "I just need to freshen up, okay? Get some cool water on my face. Use the bathroom. I'll order when I get back."

He stared at her with a doubt-filled expression on her face. Ultimately, though, he acquiesced and sat back down. She strolled calmly toward the restroom. When she finally got to the ladies' room, she rushed into one of the stalls and locked the door, as if by doing so, it might protect her from David. She sat down on the toilet, her heart beating fast, her palms sweaty. She needed to think fast. There was no way she could sneak past him to leave. What if she made a scene? There was no guarantee anyone would call the police before David dragged her out of there. Maybe if she talked to someone, another woman perhaps, here in the restroom, asked for her help…

Isobel leaned down and looked under the stall in both directions. She was alone. Surely someone would be along soon, right? Someone willing to offer assistance? Isobel sat back upright and closed her eyes. She was never one to ask for help; her pride wouldn't allow it, not when she was a teenager and not as an adult. She always believed people were unwilling to involve themselves in the lives of others, but after meeting Pastor Martin and Nancy and Karen, she learned otherwise and understood that it wasn't beyond belief that someone here would listen and offer her the help she needed.

The restroom door opened, the hinges squeaking loudly. Isobel sat up and willed herself to calm down. Her hands shook even as she settled herself upon the necessary course of action. She was going to be faithful to who she was, who she wanted to be, and she was going to ask for help.

Isobel rose to her feet and pushed the door open. An older woman walked by her to an empty stall, offering her a brief, polite smile. Isobel moved towards the sink and turned the water on. Though she washed her hands slowly, waiting for the woman to finish, Isobel was starting to grow nervous. She had already been in the bathroom for a while and was afraid David would come looking for her.

The toilet flushed. Isobel cut the faucet off and waited. She didn't have the words ready, neither was she prepared to do this, but she had to try.

The woman smiled at her again as she approached the sink. Isobel lingered at the hand dryer, hating that she was in this position.

"Ma'am," Isobel finally said.

The woman looked up at her expectantly.

"Ma'am, I'm sorry to bother you. I…" The words lodged themselves in her throat, no different than when she approached Pastor Martin for help.

"What is it, dear?" the woman asked, drying off her hands on a paper towel.

"I…I need help," Isobel finally said.

"What's wrong?"

Even though she was still hesitant, Isobel explained her situation, her fears. The woman's expression transformed from cheerful to that of distress.

"Please," Isobel added, lowering her voice as if David might hear her through the walls. "I don't want to burden you with my problem, I just need help."

"Oh my," the woman said, taking her hand. "Of course, I'll help you." Isobel relaxed her shoulders, which had been taut with stress, and sighed with relief. "You just wait here," the woman added. She stepped towards the door, a warm smile on her face. Part of Isobel wanted to truly relax, but the other part of her knew it was too early to celebrate a victory. And this was apparent when the woman opened the door and David was standing there. She jumped. Isobel did not. Not that she expected the worst, she had learned things never really worked out the way they were meant to.

Temporarily stunned, the woman backed up as David stepped inside the restroom. There was no concern, no humor in his face as he walked over to Isobel. She shrunk back against the wall, wishing she could disappear.

"Sir?" the woman stated, but he didn't even acknowledge her. Instead, he stopped just in front of Isobel and stared her down. "Sir, you can't be in here," the woman continued.

Isobel swallowed hard as she peered into his eyes. She could see a fire brewing in them.

"Sir!" the woman stated more forcefully.

"I was concerned about my wife," he said, not once looking away from Isobel.

"You need to leave."

"Once I get my wife."

"I don't think she wants to leave with you."

Isobel shut her eyes tightly, trying to block out her reality.

"She's coming with me," he responded, placing his hand on the nape of her neck. There was no gentle caress, no love. His grip was hard. Isobel felt him apply pressure, pushing her towards the door.

"Sir!"

Walking in front of him, Isobel passed the woman. She wanted to plead with her, ask her to find a way, but there was no saving her. Not now.

"Sir!" the woman called after them, as David continued walking her through the hall and into the dining room. He didn't stop at their table, but left the restaurant, leading her to his car and opening the door for her. It was only when they were seated within that his calm façade disappeared. Without warning, he threw his arm at her and struck her face with his fist. Isobel hit the window and slunk into her chair. Her face immediately felt like it was on fire, pain surging from every nerve ending in her body. Isobel nursed her head as blood dripped down her face, onto her chest.

"Dammit," he yelled, then punched the steering wheel in exasperation. "Why would you do something like that? I don't want to hurt you; can't you see that? I love you."

David hit the steering wheel again, this time sounding the horn. He said nothing else and started the engine, pulling out of the parking lot and onto the highway.

Twenty-Seven

DAVID HELD FIRMLY ONTO HER arm as he juggled their bags in one hand and pushed open the motel room door with his foot. Isobel let him drag her inside, her body deadweight as she was unwilling to help him. Her right cheek had stopped bleeding, but it was swollen now and no doubt turning a variety of colors. The left one didn't feel any better. Her face was tender where he hit her, and she knew she would have matching bruises by morning. She hadn't spoken one word to him since leaving the restaurant, and even though he expressed regret for his actions, Isobel refused to acknowledge him. There wasn't one penitent bone in his body and the moment she allowed herself to believe he might be sincere, she knew that would be her undoing. Until then, she simply needed to survive, for her child's sake, because there was no way in hell, she would allow him or her to know the pain she did.

Her determination quickly turned to panic when she realized there was only one bed in the room. She was going to have to sleep with David. She moved toward the wall, away from him. The very idea of being with him had her body trembling.

David locked the door and dropped the bags on the table. The room wasn't very big, nor was it fancy, but there wasn't much to be expected for just a few dollars a night. It was another stop off the highway, further and further away from Tory.

"You'll like the new house; the old place just wasn't the same without you," David said as he took a seat on the bed. He untied his laces and pulled his shoes off. "It's out a ways and a bit of a fixer, but it's got such great potential."

He stood up and walked over to her. Isobel shrunk back but couldn't stop him from touching her. He rested his hands on her shoulders and caressed her arms.

"I've missed you so much," he said, his voice husky. He moved closer to her. "I know things might be a little stressful with the move and this lawsuit, but we'll work through it. You'll see."

When he finally calmed down after the incident at the restaurant, David told her about his suspension and the lawsuit against him and the department. Of course, it was *her* fault. She had been gone for weeks and he just couldn't handle the situation. He snapped when a suspect mouthed off to him. David hit him once or twice, he didn't count, but the weasel accused David of wailing on him until he needed medical attention. Had she been there, this would have not happened.

Because you would have hit me instead, Isobel thought when he told her.

David raised his hand and gently touched her right cheek. Isobel winced, moving her head back away from him. Gentle became firm and David forcefully turned her head back to face him. He gazed down at her, his eyes moving between her eyes and her lips. Isobel braced herself, knowing what was coming. When he leaned down and kissed her, she shut her eyes, pursed her lips defiantly, and turned her head.

This only served to make him mad. David grabbed her jaw and turned her back to him. He kissed her hard, forcing her mouth open. Refusing to respond to him, Isobel pushed away from him again, taking a couple steps to her right. She expected him to be upset, but he remained calm.

He took two steps closer to her. She took another one and found there was nowhere else to go. She had trapped herself into the corner. He continued approaching her until they were a mere hair apart.

"You were the one who said you wanted to come," he said with frightful composure.

"Because you would have hurt me otherwise," she responded, swallowing hard.

David brought a hand up, smoothing her hair back behind her ears—something Tory liked to do. It didn't feel the same now.

"I would never hurt you," he seemed to promise, his eyes on his hand. He let her hair slip through his fingers.

"But...you have," she said, her voice wavering.

"I didn't mean to."

Isobel sighed. He didn't nor would he ever understand.

"I don't ever want you to fear me, Isobel..."

She opened her mouth to argue, but he interrupted with a hand to her mouth.

"I don't want to hurt you. I don't want to do anything to make you even think about leaving. Because if you do, then there's no telling what I'll do or who I'll have to hurt to get you back."

Though he offered no names, Isobel knew whom he meant—Tory. Her heart fell. She could never go back to him without putting him in danger.

"Am I clear, Isobel? Do you understand?"

She nodded.

"Yes, what?" he asked.

"Yes, I understand. I'm not going to go anywhere."

The words were difficult to say, but she had no choice. If she left, if she ever left, she'd be risking Tory's life. It was enough the pain she put him through already. She could never forgive herself if David hurt him.

"I just want for us to be happy, like we used to be," he said, taking her hands in his. "Can we do that? Can we go back to how it used to be?"

Though it killed her to do it, Isobel nodded her head once more. It was the only choice she had right then and there. Eventually her options would be harder and fewer, if not non-existent. But that wasn't something she could worry about now.

"Good," David stated, lifting her chin with his finger. "Go get ready for bed."

Isobel waited for him to step aside before slowly tiptoeing to her bag. Tears pooled at the corners of her eyes as she searched for her pajamas and toiletries. Beyond the regret and the guilt, Isobel was tired of feeling and she took her time showering and dressing. She dreaded what was coming next and put it off as much as possible.

Calm yourself, she thought, gazing at her reflection in the mirror. *This isn't anything you haven't done before. Just stay calm and everything will be okay.*

Isobel took a deep breath and stepped out of the bathroom. David was in bed already, wearing only his briefs. Clearing her mind, she placed her clothes and bag on the table and walked over to the bed, taking a seat on the edge opposite of him. She tried willing herself to lie down beside him, but it seemed every part of her was fighting it. She didn't want David, she wanted Tory. She wanted his touch, his love. He made her feel special, unique, adored, cherished, and beloved.

The bed moved, and David came up behind her. He pulled her down beside him. Eyes shut tight, Isobel swallowed hard and did what she could to stop the tears that were forming anew, especially when David began kissing her neck. She wanted to recoil from his touch, but forced herself to stay put, knowing things would go worse for her if she fought him. Isobel kept her eyes closed and thought about Tory, about their morning together, earlier that day.

Ever the morning person, Isobel was the first to wake. She kept her own bedroom but spent the night with Tory every night. He had ravished her the night before, bringing her to such pleasurable heights, she was still reeling from them that morning. Yet, there was something to be said for intimacy, pure and simple. Being with someone and not having to do anything more than to be in the same room with them. To breathe in their air. To feel their presence. And as she awoke that morning, the sunlight streaming in through the blinds, illuminating his sleeping form, Tory was her world. He was all she knew, all she wanted to know.

She rolled over onto her side and watched him as he slept. His dark hair was mussed up, still shaggy, still in need of a haircut, but oh so cute. His beard had filled in, though he continued to keep it short and trimmed. He had one arm tucked underneath his pillow while the other rested on top of it. He was unclothed, as was she, allowing her to appreciate his body—strong arms, firm shoulders, and a solid chest. He had some chest hair, but it was fine and soft to the touch; she loved to weave her fingers through it. His skin was fairer than hers, but she loved the feel of it, the color, and the look. Words couldn't truly express what she felt for him in that moment.

Then he opened his eyes, his beautiful green eyes, and she wanted to believe that what she felt for him was being reflected back to her. As he lifted his arm and rolled back onto his side, gazing at her with those eyes, so exotic and addicting, Isobel lost her train of thought. She was content to be there, beside him, being the banquet his eyes feasted on.

Tory brought his hand up to her face and caressed her cheek, his touch soft. He moved closer to her, their bodies touching now, as his hand covered her neck, her shoulders, and her arms. Isobel closed her eyes, relishing how he made her feel with so simple an action.

The bed moved underneath them, and Isobel felt as Tory gently guided her onto her back. She opened her eyes just long enough to see him leaning into her. Her eyes coasted shut as his lips traced hers. She opened her mouth and invited him in, their tongues touching, dueling, clashing, mating. Isobel brought her hands up to his face and stroked his cheeks. She loved the feel of the short stubble on her palms. Over her arms and down her hips his hand traveled, causing her to shudder. Without thought to his needs, Tory found the entrance to her passion and stroked her, slow, methodically, then fast and reckless, pushing her higher and higher till she could go no further. She fell off the peak he had brought her to, right into his arms.

But he gave her no time to relax; before she could still her pounding heart, Tory entered her and took her back up to that peak.

His touch, inside and out, was electrifying; and she couldn't help her reaction to him. She cried out and encouraged him to continue; and when he himself reached that same apex, she pulled him close to her, so that they were as one, her heart beating with his. She never felt closer to Tory than she did in that moment—and never more farther away than she did right now.

Isobel opened her eyes as David grunted and rolled off of her, having expended himself. She sighed, and pulled her shirt down, stretching it as far as it would go, trying to cover herself once more. She wiped his sweat off of her, but she couldn't remove his stench from her nostrils or the sense of filth he left her with. Isobel turned her back to him as he settled in for the night and pulled the comforter over her head, praying sleep would find her quickly.

Twenty-Eight

SLEEP EVADED ISOBEL. AFTER tossing and turning for hours, she got up to shower again. She turned the water as hot as she could stand it and let it run over her. Though the cut on her face had closed, it still hurt. She avoided the area as she washed up, scrubbing hard the parts where David touched her, letting the hot water rinse off his dirtiness. It wasn't until the water ran cold that she finally got out. She wrapped a towel around her and sat on the edge of the tub. She needed to get dressed but could hardly make herself move. Her limbs felt heavier, grounding her where she sat, numbing the part of her soul that cared.

When she heard David stirring, Isobel rose and forced herself to get ready. She applied make-up to the bruises on her face, once more covering up for David's sins. It was easier, though, than trying to explain what happened. She did what she could, gathered her items and exited the bathroom. She put her things together, ignoring David as he grabbed his things to shower up. She started to worry when she heard him run off a string of expletives, presumably because the water was running cold, but the part of her that was numb didn't care. She busied herself with tidying up the room then sat down at the table to wait for David.

Isobel turned on the television and flipped through the news stations, looking for a distraction. She should have been getting ready for work, getting ready to start her new career as a chef, but instead, she was running once again, leaving behind the people who cared for and took a chance on her. Would Karen believe she had simply relapsed into her former ways? What about Nancy? How much heartache would this cause her once Pastor Martin shared the news with her? And the man of God himself? He was meddlesome, but in a good way. He cared. And this was his reward: he would forever believe she had ignored his advice.

She didn't get a chance to pity herself too much more, as David stepped out of the bathroom. He looked upset.

"You'd think with all the money these dumps make they could put in a decent water heater," he muttered as he got dressed.

Happy for a reprieve, Isobel turned back to the television and waited for him to finish getting ready. Once he had collected his things, David walked over to the table and sat beside her. He reached up and gently—*no, lightly,* she corrected herself, as there was nothing gentle about the man—touched her face. She flinched.

"I know we got off to a rough start, but it'll get better," he promised.

Isobel simply nodded. Not in agreement though; she just wanted to keep the peace.

"Come on. We need to get some gas before we grab breakfast. Then we'll head home."

She didn't even consider the thoughts that word evoked, focusing instead on the numbness that had invaded her heart. Isobel obeyed and a couple of hours later they were on the road, headed to the place she would now reside. She remained quiet through much of the ride, choosing to watch the scenery as they drove by.

Mid-morning, they heard a police siren behind them. David cursed as he checked the rearview mirror—they were being pulled over. Isobel looked around briefly to see it was an unmarked vehicle following them.

"Don't say a word," David warned her as he pulled over onto the shoulder. Once he parked, he grabbed the registration from the glove compartment and his insurance card from his wallet to expedite the process.

Isobel watched him, his guilt apparent. Could she use this to her advantage? She turned around, wondering if she should even dare when her breath hitched in her throat and she whispered, "Rebecca."

TORY WATCHED as Rebecca approached the vehicle in front of them. When she told him about a couple of leads she had on Harris, including a police report filed by a woman at a restaurant who described Isobel, Tory insisted on coming along. He was up all night worrying about Isobel and letting his mind go places it shouldn't—like what he would do to Harris once they found him. He wasn't normally a violent man, but the thought of Isobel being hurt by this man was enough to drive him to murder.

Rebecca, of course, knew this and argued that he had no place going with her, but he begged and appealed to her heart, knowing he couldn't sit at home and wait any longer. For the sake of their friendship, she finally agreed, but she made him promise to adhere to her command. If he went off on his own agenda, she warned, she would shoot him herself. Tory gave her his word: he would be on his best behavior. He would remain in the car as she did her job. He simply wanted Isobel back.

Seeing his wife now in the front seat of Harris' car, Tory felt some of his agitation leave him—but not all of it. Anxious to have her back with him, he opened the door and stepped out of the car. He wouldn't approach until Rebecca gave him permission to do so, but he was ready.

Unfortunately, Rebecca didn't get a chance to say or do anything. She barely made it to the driver's side before Harris forcefully threw open his door, knocking her to the ground. Tory gasped, then realized she was in the path of an oncoming car. Without hesitation, Tory ran over to her as Harris drove off. He grabbed her jacket and pulled her into his arms and out of the way of the other car. They rolled onto the other side of the highway as tires screeched and the acrid smell of burning rubber filled the air. The other car barely missed them before coming to a stop on the shoulder.

Everything went silent for a moment. Tory didn't move, his arms protectively around Rebecca. He looked her over quickly to make sure she had no injuries.

"Are you okay?" he asked.

Rebecca shook him off of her.

"Dammit, Tory, I told you to stay in the car," she said sternly.

Tory refrained from commenting and returned to the vehicle with haste. He was still fastening his seatbelt when she threw the car in drive and gave chase. Even with his belt on though, Tory found himself being tossed from side-to-side. With the sirens blaring, Rebecca called for back-up. Cars ahead of them made way as their speeds increased and the pursuit escalated.

Within minutes, more sirens were heard behind them: another police car joined in the chase. Harris continued weaving through traffic, making no effort to slow down or avoid any of the cars around him. He plowed through them like a bowling ball through pins. Several drivers braked quickly, causing the cars behind them to slam into each other.

Fear gripped Tory's heart; someone was going to get hurt, and sadly, that would be the best-case scenario.

Traffic became denser, making it more difficult for Harris to maintain his speed. Tory breathed with relief as they slowed down, but Rebecca only cursed. They were approaching an off-ramp—Harris intended to take the chase off the highway. Rebecca slowed down as Harris banked to the right to veer around a tractor-trailer. He didn't slow down though and lost control of his vehicle, plowing right into the guard rail and bringing the chase to an abrupt end.

Rebecca moved onto the shoulder and slammed on her brakes, lurching both of them forward. Before the car came to a complete stop, Tory threw open the door and ran towards the wreck.

"Tory, wait!" she called out, but he couldn't stop, not now. He needed to get to Isobel. He needed to know she was still alive. He reached the car and noted how the front end was tangled up with the rail. He tried the passenger door, but the frame was dented inward, the windows shattered. Glass was everywhere. Inside the car, Isobel was leaning over the center console of the car; he couldn't tell if she was breathing or not as her seatbelt was still fastened, holding her body back in the chair.

He fought to get the door open but couldn't get the metal to budge. Rebecca ran up behind him and together they were able to move it enough for him to squeeze through. But for all his experience working in the ER, with life-and-death situations, Tory found he couldn't act. Seeing her there in the car, broken and battered, all he could think about was how much he had failed her. He was the reason she was there, the reason she was hurt. He didn't abuse her like David did, but when everything was said and done, Tory was just as bad; he used her, enjoyed her body, but always kept her at a distance, always left her emotionally detached. He was supposed to protect her, love her, and cherish her. She was his wife after all.

My wife, he thought. Mrs. Isobel Jamison. His other half, his completion. All of sudden, none of the other things mattered, not that she left, not that she took up with another man, not that she failed to mention her pregnancy for two months. He had gone after her to make sure she was safe, unwilling to lose her like this. Seeing her now in the car though, understanding what she meant to him, Tory decided he couldn't lose her at all.

"Tory."

Rebecca's voice coaxed him back to the present situation, reminding him that he had the ability to fix Isobel.

As Rebecca called for paramedics, Tory reached up and checked Isobel for a pulse. It was weak, but her heart was still pounding and that was good. He looked her over to make sure there weren't any life-threatening injuries. There were none, as far as he could tell. It might be a whole different story from the inside, but he wouldn't know till she got to a hospital. And he certainly couldn't move her no matter how much wanted to take her into his arms and care for her—that would have to wait until the paramedics arrived.

Holding her hand in his, he moved her hair back off her face, revealing a cut and darkly colored bruise on her right cheek. He was going to dismiss it as a result of the accident until he realized the cut had scabbed over: she had acquired it *beforehand*.

Just then, a groan escaped from the driver's side of the car. Tory looked up as Detective Harris began stirring. Like Isobel, he was still fastened into the car by his seat belt, but he bore only a few cuts on his forehead and temple. Slowly, the man sat up, holding his head in his hands. He seemed dazed, lost even as he looked around him. When Harris met Tory's gaze though, all confusion left him. As fast as his body would allow him, he released his belt and pushed open his door.

Fury consumed Tory. He let go of Isobel and went after Harris, pushing Rebecca back. The man ran when he saw Tory behind him, but he was still stunned from the accident. He stumbled a few feet from the car and dropped to the ground. Before he could regain his footing, Tory pounced on him and pinned him to the ground. He grabbed him by the lapels of his jacket and threatened him: "Let's see how you like it when you get hit."

Tory let go of his coat, then punched him hard in the face. The detective didn't fight back, didn't offer any resistance. Tory knew it wasn't a fair fight, but he wasn't interested in being just or reasonable—he wanted blood. He wanted revenge for what the man had done to Isobel. Hit for hit, blow for blow, let him hurt the way he had hurt her; let him feel fear the way he caused her to fear.

Harris' face was a bloody mess by the time Rebecca pulled Tory off of him.

"Tory, stop!"

He struggled with her hold on him, but she wouldn't release him.

"Don't do this," she pleaded. "He's not worth it,"

While he was strong, Rebecca proved to be much stronger. She swept his feet out from under him and had him on his knees in seconds. His will to fight left him and as he watched Harris now, who was far from the presence Tory once thought he was, Tory knew she was right: Harris had done enough to them, Tory would give him no more.

Twenty-Nine

TORY HELPED OUT AS MUCH AS he could, not just with Isobel, but also with the other drivers involved in the prior collisions. When the paramedics arrived though, he stayed out of the way as they did their job. Little-by-little the scene of the accident was cleared up. Isobel was taken to the hospital, as was Harris, who would be treated and then arrested. Tory wanted to leave with his wife, but he chose to stay behind to talk to Rebecca. He owed her an apology.

When the ambulances left, he sat down on the shoulder next to Rebecca's car and watched as she finished up. Other officers arrived to help and between all of them, the area was vacated in no time. Broken glass was the only indicator that anything had occurred.

After the last of the police left, Rebecca returned to her car to leave as well. She seemed surprised to see him, but not annoyed, which was good since she was his ride.

She wandered over and sat down beside him.

"I should kick your ass for not listening to me," she said, with a big smile.

"I saved your life," he playfully retorted.

"Ha! Seems to me I was the only one doing any saving around here, while you were—"

"In the way," he finished, coloring his tone with regret.

"Yeah, you were. But since this was your first 'ride-along', I'll let it slide."

Tory laughed, appreciative of her good nature. It reminded him of all the things that made her a great person and made him pursue her in the first place. He sighed, thinking about how he continued breaking promise after promise to her.

"Listen, Rebecca," he began, making purposeful eye contact with her. "I'm sorry. You were gracious enough to let me come even though it was against the rules and I acted like a complete idiot."

She chuckled at him.

"It's alright, Tory. Given the situation, I don't blame you. And to be honest, you showed more restraint than most."

He laughed. "You're too kind."

"Nah, just tired. It's been a long two days." Tory nodded in agreement. "And thank you. For jumping in like you did. You did save my life."

Tory smiled.

"Come on, let's get you to the hospital," she said.

Before she could stand, Tory took her hand and said, "Thank you for everything. I'll never be able to repay you."

She pulled her hand back and waved him off.

"Just call me and let me know how Isobel and the baby are doing. Then we'll be even."

He understood the implication of her request. So often police officers, like doctors, helped people, never knowing how they fared out. It was nice to know happy endings did exist. But there was also other side of what she was asking: she meant to not see him again, beyond what their jobs required. He didn't know if they would remain friends or not, but at least they were parting on good terms.

"I will," he said.

They were on the road again in minutes and at the hospital in no time. Rebecca reminded him to call her once he had news, then she left. Inside the waiting room, Tory found Pastor Martin doing just that— waiting. He had called the minister earlier to let him know what happened, and the man was only too happy to meet him at the hospital. And not just him, but also his parents. Tory was surprised to see them there, his mother especially.

"Tory!" his mother said, embracing him.

"What are you doing here?" he asked her.

"What kind of question is that?" she replied indignantly.

"Pastor Martin called us," his father interjected. "He told us what happened with Isobel."

This still didn't answer his question, but Tory figured now was not the time to push for answers. Deep down inside though, Tory knew the truth: whether worrying about him succumbing to the wiles of a wayward woman or stressing because he had accompanied the police in a high-speed chase to get his wife back, Sarah Jamison would always be there for him. And after spending the last two days worrying about Isobel, Tory couldn't help but appreciate her devotion. He resolved to do better when it came to talking to her and including her in his life.

First things first, though.

"How's Isobel?" Tory asked.

"They're still treating her," his dad said.

Tory nodded and took a seat. While he always felt comfortable in hospitals and doctors' offices, he found he was too antsy and too nervous to find peace today, the circumstances being what they were. What if

Isobel received permanent injuries? What if there was internal bleeding? What if there were complications? What if she died? What if her child died? What if they were both gone? What if...

"Dr. Ramirez," his mother stated as she stood up. Tory followed her gaze to the short Latin doctor approaching them and quickly rose to his feet, everyone else following suit.

"It's always good to see you, Sarah," he said, a warm smile on his face, as he shook her hand. The two had worked together at the hospital before his mother retired.

"And you, Benito. How are you?"

Tory sighed impatiently. Now was not the time to catch up.

"How's Isobel?" Tory interjected, cutting their chit-chat short.

Dr. Ramirez turned to him and replied, "She's got a concussion and her spleen ruptured. We had to go in to stop the bleeding. Other than that, her injuries are minor, and she'll recover. She's out of surgery now and resting."

"And the baby?" Tory asked.

"Baby? What baby?" Sarah demanded. "What are you talking about?"

Apparently, Pastor Martin didn't mention everything. Tory was going to have a lot of explaining to do.

Later.

"Dr. Ramirez?" he pleaded.

The man smiled.

"She's fine; got a strong heartbeat and the placenta remains attached to the uterus. You'll need to schedule an appointment with Isobel's primary and watch for any vaginal bleeding, leaking fluid, contractions or other abdominal pain."

Tory released the breath he had been holding. Isobel and her daughter were fine.

Her daughter. Isobel was having a girl. Tory felt curiously excited.

"Come on. I'll take you to see her," Dr. Ramirez said.

Tory started following. They hadn't gone very far when he realized no one else was moving. Not even his mother, though she did continue arguing.

"Go on, son. We'll be here," his father said as he wrapped his arms around his wife.

Tory nodded appreciatively, then continued after the doctor, anxiety creeping into his heart with every step they took. This was the moment he had been anticipating since Isobel left the first time, the dream he had of being reunited with her. Of looking past what had been and moving into a future they could both be a part of. He had almost screwed it up, but he was going to make it right now. He was going to say all the things he should have told her to start with and pray she accepted him.

With that thought, Tory took a deep breath and relaxed as they arrived at Isobel's room.

"Just grab one of the nurses if you need anything."

"Thank you, Dr. Ramirez," he said and pushed past the curtain inside the room.

Isobel lay on the bed, sleeping. He watched as her chest rose and fell with every breath she took. A sheet covered her body from her chest down, outlining her form and defining her rounded belly, the one he had so blatantly missed. How could he be so blind to what was so obvious?

Tory grabbed a chair as he approached the bed and seated himself right next to her. He reached out and gently caressed her arm, resting his head beside her. Tory listened to the constant beat of her heart monitor, to the steady rhythm of her breathing; and soon fell asleep.

THE MOVEMENT was subtle, but enough to wake Tory. He raised his head and saw Isobel stirring. Her eyes gradually opened. She seemed lost, uncertain.

"Hey," he said softly. Ever so gently, Tory pushed her hair back. Her eyes focused and she gazed at him. Isobel swallowed hard and grimaced. He let go of her long enough to get her a cup of water; then he helped her sit up and drink. When she finished, he set the cup back down and picked her hand up again.

"You're pretty banged up, but you're going to be alright. You and your daughter."

Isobel's eyes widened at the news. Until then, Tory had no idea whether or not she knew the gender of her child and he was glad to be the one to tell her.

"She's strong. Just like her mom," he added.

At that, her face flushed, and her eyes misted over. Her hand tightened into a fist and she pulled her arm away from him.

"Tory." Her voice was hoarse. "Tory…"

He saw the difficulty with which she spoke, the unease in her countenance and the tension in her muscles. Whatever she wanted to say was stressing her and that was the last thing she needed. Using a soothing tone, he encouraged her to rest.

"Shh. We can talk later."

She shook her head.

"Tory, I should have told you sooner, but I didn't want to hurt you more than I already had and…I was scared you wouldn't forgive me if you knew…"

She was apologizing. After all he said and did yesterday…

"Isobel, don't—"

"Leaving you was the biggest mistake I ever made. You were the only thing in my life that made sense and I threw it away because I was afraid. I felt stuck, trapped, not because of you, but because I didn't know who I was. I didn't know how to be your wife. I never wanted to hurt you, Tory. Please believe me."

He shook his head.

"Isobel—"

"I want to be with you. I want to stay with you. You're the only one I want. Last night"—she hung her head—"last night …with David, I didn't want to, but I had no choice."

Tory understood the implication of her words, but he didn't want to think about that right now. He started to caress her face, to tell her to stop, that they would talk about it later, when he took her home with him, but she raised her head and met his gaze. "Will you forgive me? Please?"

Tory saw the pain in her eyes and the shame weighing her down. That he had finally and truly forgiven her was irrelevant: she needed to hear him say it. She needed his reassurance to know that he had let it go…and that she could too.

"I forgive you," he said and watched as she visibly relaxed. He sighed and continued, "Now, will you forgive me? I reacted to your news badly. I was hurting, and wanted you to hurt, even though you were right. I used you. I took and took from you, but I never gave back. And I put you in danger because I was too damned scared to open myself up to you again. You were the only happiness I ever knew, and I don't want us to be apart anymore. I want to be husband and wife again. Not because you're a great cook or you keep my home clean, but because I love you. Because you are my better half. Because I am complete when you're with me." Tears streamed down his face as he spoke, but he made no effort to wipe them away. "We've already done the 'for worse' part; can we give 'for better' a try? I don't know what will happen, but I don't want to live another day without you. I love you, Isobel."

She was crying now as well. She didn't have to say it for him to know it: she had forgiven him.

Isobel smiled and whispered, "I love you, Tory."

Remembering how he reacted the last time she spoke those words, Tory kissed her and said, "I know. I know you do."

He touched his forehead to hers, his heart racing with joy. They still had a lot to work through, a lot to talk about, but this was a good start. This was the perfect start. Or it would be as soon as she said yes.

"So, what do you say Isobel? Will you marry me? Again? Will you let me be your husband? Let me take care of you and your daughter? Let me be her father?"

Her gaze softened up and she relaxed completely.

"Yes," she whispered.

Though he wanted to hold her, he didn't want to bring her any further discomfort following her surgery. So, he contented himself with gently touching any part of her in his reach—her arm, her face, her belly. With his hand resting on her bump, Tory felt a slight quiver and marveled at the miracle. Not just the baby, but his life as well. Where he had been single just the day before, he had his wife back now and they were going to be parents of a little girl in just a few short months.

And what a busy few months they were going to be as Isobel recovered and they renewed their vows. They had to prepare for the baby and buy all the things she would need. They also had to move Isobel into his bedroom—no, *their* bedroom—and set up a nursery in the other one. Or maybe they would move, someplace bigger, with a yard for *their* daughter to play in. They were going to have to choose a name...

Tory perked up as an idea struck him.

"Hey, can we call her Hannah?"

Isobel gazed at him with amusement; then she smiled and said, "I think the name is perfect."

He kissed her lips gently and rested his head beside hers, speaking tenderly to her.

Read on for the first chapter of
THE BOOK OF JOY

Shannon wants for nothing except the love of a good woman. However, he is so focused on his career and caring for his elderly mother Evelyn, he doesn't realize he's missing anything. Until he meets Joya, the widowed daughter-in-law of a family friend. She is a loving, generous woman who brings a much-needed spark into his life; but because she is younger than him and still dealing with the loss of her husband, he is hesitant to approach her.

Joya, for her part, maintains a good attitude about her situation and is appreciative of the people around her—especially Shannon, whose friendship fills the gaps in her life that would otherwise remain empty. But after burying her husband, she isn't sure she has it in her to fall in love again.

This, of course, will not do for Evelyn, who sees the potential for love (and grandchildren) in them. Nor for Gail, the family friend, who has her own reasons for wanting to match the two. They go to great lengths to bring Shannon and Joya together. But as the four contend with the directions their lives are moving, they soon discover that sometimes life is more about letting yourself be loved than it is about falling into it.

One

VELYN BARTON REECE DID not consider herself a nosy neighbor. She was curious, concerned even, but not nosy. So, when she heard the sound of a school bus coming to a stop at the end of her street, she knew something was off. She paused the telephone conversation she was having with her friend Gail, then marched over to the window to investigate. There were several children in the neighborhood, ranging from kindergarten to high school. Most of the older kids rode the bus home, none of the younger ones did.

As a concerned neighbor, she knew this.

"Hold on," Evelyn advised her friend, as she reached the window, a little out of breath. As a septuagenarian, she had long passed the prime of her life. She had also passed her ideal weight decades earlier and was on the heavier side of the scale. However, a person only lived but so long, and life—and food— had to be enjoyed. This was the maxim she lived by and damn, if it hadn't led to a good, enjoyable life.

"What's wrong?" she heard Gail say, but Evelyn gave no response. She pulled aside the curtain and watched as the school bus opened its door. She didn't see anyone get off, but then the kids were small, and her eyes weren't as sharp as they used to be. Still, just to be on the safe side, she waited until the bus drove off before deciding nothing was wrong. It was then she spied a young girl, about five years of age, skipping to her house. Evelyn recognized her as the daughter of the new neighbor she had only briefly met. She thought it odd that the mother, who worked full-time, would be home at this hour, but Evelyn wasn't keen to her schedule. Still, she continued watching and found her curiosity was justified when the little girl walked up to her front door and turned the knob, only to discover it was locked. She tried the side door but found no one was home. Perplexed by the situation, the little girl just stood there.

"Gail, I'm gonna have to call you back," Evelyn said. Without waiting for a response, she hit the off button on the phone and set it on the table. Then she lumbered to the door and opened the screen far enough so that she didn't have to venture too far out. It wasn't officially summer yet, but the days were hot, and sticky.

"Hey," she yelled out, trying to get the little girl's attention, but to no avail. The girl continued staring at her house, as if trying to will someone to open the door.

"Hey, little girl," Evelyn called again, a little louder this time, as she swatted a fly attempting entry into her house. "Little girl!"

The child finally looked over towards her.

"Come here," Evelyn yelled, impatiently waving her hand towards her.

Still, the girl hesitated.

Evelyn let out a noisy sigh. She knew she wasn't making a very inviting impression on the girl, but she couldn't leave her standing out there by herself.

"Come here, child," she said with more force in her voice.

The girl vacillated for a moment longer before finally deciding to walk over. She cut through the adjacent neighbor's yard and arrived at Evelyn's doorstep in no time.

"What's your name, child?" the older woman asked.

"Hannah Myers," she replied, matter-of-factly. She squinted as she looked up at Evelyn. She was a beautiful girl, with large, round, curious eyes and black, curly hair that fell onto her face. Though her skin was the color of rich caramel, much lighter than Evelyn's dark brown tone, her features—nose, hair texture—were that of a black child. Mixed parentage, the older woman figured, no different than her son, Jackie.

"What are you doing home?" Evelyn

demanded, getting back to the topic at hand. "You don't normally catch the bus."

With an attitude befitting someone much older than her, Hannah placed her hands on her hips and replied, "I wanted to come home."

Evelyn glared back at her, surprised to hear such a tone come out of a small package.

"But you don't get to decide that, especially when your mother isn't home," she said.

"Well, I didn't want to go to after-school," Hannah returned, her eyes fixed on Evelyn, almost daring her to argue.

Evelyn marveled at her gumption. She had never met such a strong-willed child in her life and wasn't sure if she should be annoyed or impressed. Still, there was no excuse for the youngster to go out on her own and as the little girl's elder and neighbor, Evelyn had a responsibility to make sure Hannah was safe. She swung open the door to allow the little girl entrance.

"Come on in."

Hannah hesitated.

"What now?" Evelyn asked.

"I'm not supposed to go with strangers."

The child was strong-willed and smart— probably too smart for her own good.

"Well, I'm not a stranger, I'm your

neighbor."

"I don't know your name."

"Evelyn," she replied and extended her hand.

Hannah took hold of it and shook it.

"Now come inside before I get a house full of bugs," Evelyn insisted. Hannah didn't hesitate this time and entered. She had never been in the house before, but it didn't stop her from walking around like she knew where she was going. Evelyn stared at her curiously before closing the front door and following her into the kitchen.

"Can I have a snack?" Hannah asked, gazing up at the refrigerator.

Humored by the little girls' forwardness, Evelyn replied, "Sure. Have a seat."

The little girl removed her backpack and promptly obeyed. While Evelyn made her a sandwich (peanut butter and honey, as requested), Hannah peppered her with questions.

"Why is your hair white? Why do you have hair on your chin? Why is your house so old? Do you have any pets? Do you have any kids I can play with? Can I have some juice?"

Apparently, they were all rhetorical, because she kept right on talking.

"You look like my Grandma Wilma. She doesn't have white hair, but she's brown like you. Grandma Margery is peach like my mommy, not brown like you, and sometimes I stay with her when Mommy is working. She doesn't like my daddy. She said he's a loser and she's glad he's gone, but she likes Grandma Wilma, who calls me a lot and sends me letters in the mail. I'm going to see her in the summer. I'm gonna fly in an airplane and I'm gonna have fun with her. Can you cut my sandwich in half like my mommy does? It tastes better like that…"

Hannah was not a shy child; and Evelyn was enjoying her company, even if it was accidental…which reminded her.

"What's your mom's name?" Evelyn asked, finally able to get a word in edge-wise as Hannah started eating.

"Ashley Myers, but I'm not allowed to call her by her grown-up name—"

Evelyn interrupted her.

"Does your mom have a cell phone?"

"Yes. Sometimes she lets me play on it—"

Evelyn had to cut her off again.

"Alright sweetie, do you know her number? We need to call her to let her know you're here."

"She made me memorize it in case I got separated from her," Hannah stated, then gave Evelyn the number. While the little girl continued eating, Evelyn dialed. A young woman's voice greeted her.

"Are you Hannah's mom?" Evelyn asked.

There was a pause, followed by a sigh.

"What happened now?"

Evelyn reintroduced herself, then explained why she was calling. The woman immediately went from hesitant to frantic. She thanked Evelyn profusely and promised to leave immediately to pick-up her daughter.

"Don't rush and get yourself into an accident. She's fine. Just eating now, so take your time."

"I don't want to trouble you any further."

"Nonsense. It's no trouble. I don't mind the company. An old woman like me doesn't get too many visitors."

"Thank you, Ms. Evelyn."

"You're welcome," the older woman said and hung up. Then she sat down opposite of Hannah and listened as the little girl continued talking. The topics varied, but not her enthusiasm. She was energetic and animated as she talked. Evelyn couldn't help but smile. She didn't have grandchildren of her own, but she imagined this is what it would be like—talking, having fun, enjoying each other's company. Hannah was a good fill-in for right now, but oh, what joy that would be, if she had her own granddaughter.

Unfortunately, at the rate Jackie, her only child, was going, Evelyn was never going to realize that dream. He was fifty-years-old and though he was still young in her eyes, he was older than most single men out there looking for a potential spouse. At this point, Evelyn was happy to give up her old-fashioned standards if he chose to simply procreate. Regrettably, he wasn't even willing to do that. It wasn't fair to the child, he told her, to the mother or to him. Apparently, Evelyn and her husband had done *too* good of a job raising him...

Dammit, she thought.

The doorbell rang.

"Mommy!" Hannah shrieked and jumped up from the table.

"Hold on, Missy," Evelyn stated, pulling Hannah's attention back to her. She held her hand out to the little girl and said, "Here, help me up and we'll go see who's at the door together, okay?"

Hannah complied and took her hand. Evelyn stood up, her old back creaking and cracking in various places. Together they walked to the door, Hannah still holding onto her hand. Evelyn's heart melted a little.

"Mommy!" the little girl shrieked again when Evelyn opened the door.

A young woman stood there, a frenzied

look on her face. She hugged her daughter then asked, "What were you thinking getting on that bus?"

"I was ready to go home," Hannah replied matter-of-factly.

The woman sucked in a deep breath and through gritted teeth, said, "We'll talk about it when we get home. Where's your book-bag?"

"In the kitchen. I'll get it," the little girl stated and ran off to get it.

Evelyn smiled as she watched her go.

"Thank you again," Ashley said to the older woman. "Hannah's always had a strong will. It gets her in trouble and keeps me busy."

"It's alright, child. I'm glad to have helped out. And listen, if you need someone to watch her, just call me. You have my number now. Not too often, I'm an old woman, but I'll do what I can."

Ashley offered an appreciative grin then focused on Hannah as she came bounding back into the living room.

"Did you thank Ms. Evelyn?" her mother asked her.

Hannah grabbed Evelyn around the waist and hugged her.

"Thank you, Ms. Evelyn. See you later," she said, nonchalantly, as if their visit had been a planned one. Then she left, skipping alongside her mom as they walked to their house.

Evelyn felt good for having helped, but as she closed the door, she couldn't help the ache that crept into her heart. She wanted to believe she could still become a grandmother, but the truth was, with circumstances being what they were, it was much too late for that.

Yeah, right, Evelyn chuckled to herself as she wandered back into the kitchen. There might be an ache in her heart, but as long as there was breath in her body, it was never too late.

Acknowledgements

A big thank you to my family, my editor, my beta readers and all the folks who continue to believe in me. This book and all the others I've written would not have come to life without your love, your support and your assistance. And for that I am grateful.

About the Author

Ruth E. Griffin could draw pictures before she could put sentences together. Eventually, though, she figured out how to do both and is now the author of several books (fiction and non-fiction) which center on women's experiences. She still designs but focuses all her free time on writing. Ruth currently lives in North Carolina with her husband and three children. Her work is available at major online bookstores, while new book release and event information can be found at www.ruthegriffin.com. Email her at ruthegriffin@outlook.com.

Ruth E. Griffin